September 1860

America is coming apart at the seams. Tensions are high throughout the country, even in the state of Wisconsin, admitted to the Union just 12 years earlier. The issue of slavery, and the abolition of it, is on every adult's mind.

10 year-old Mary Anne Fahey, however, is not thinking about slavery at all. She is excited that she will be taking a ride on a side-wheel steamship, the *Lady Elgin*, from Milwaukee to Chicago, where her father Patrick, her mother Mary, her friend Willie, and his dad, Captain Garrett Barry, will all be participating in a parade and attending a rally for Stephen Douglas, the Democrat from Illinois who is running for President against the Republican candidate, Abraham Lincoln.

Mary Anne and Willie have no idea that they are about to become part of the largest tragedy to ever occur on Lake Michigan. The *Lady Elgin,* already considered by some to be cursed, is about to go down in history for the greatest loss of life on the waters of the Great Lakes. Who will survive?

Lost Lady is based on the true story of the disaster that rocked a nation already in the throes of discord and conflict. The events leading to this horrific tragedy, along with the heroic attempts both on land and sea to save the lives of so many, is an account worthy of tribute to the heroes and in deference to all those who perished on that fateful night.

Lost Lady

The Lady Elgin Tragedy

By M. Paul Hollander

To any family who lost a loved one on the Lady Elgin,
especially those that wondered (or still wonder) what became
of their relative.

Chapter 1

September 6, 1860

6 P.M.

"Mary Anne, hurry up! We need to get down to the dock."

"Coming, Mommy. I'm just putting on my necklace."

Her mother, Mary Fahey, gave an exasperated sigh. "You will be the death of me, young lady." Still, as she watched 10 year-old Mary Anne come into the parlor, a proud smile crossed her face. "You look very nice, Mary Anne. That necklace looks very beautiful on you."

"Thanks, Mom," her daughter replied. "I wanted to look nice for our trip to Chicago on the *Lady Elgin*." She grinned over at her two younger brothers, William, age 8, and Charles Patrick, age 4.

"Why does Mary Anne get to go to Chicago?" whined William. "I want to go too."

"Me, too!" piped in Charles, not really sure what was going on, but just as eager as his older brother to join in the family excursion.

Mary Fahey smiled down at her two young boys and gently shook her head. "Now you two know that your Uncle Michael and Aunt Mary are going to watch you. You get to play with your cousins. Don't you think that will be fun?"

William was not placated. "Yeah, but Mary Anne gets to go on the boat. That's not fair."

"Now, William," his mother scolded, "you will have your chance another time. For now, your aunt and uncle are waiting for you outside. Get along now."

The two boys obediently headed out the door and into the 3rd Ward, an Irish community in the heart of Milwaukee, Wisconsin. The Fahey family lived on Milwaukee Street, between Huron and Michigan Streets, just a few blocks from Lake Michigan. It was a rough neighborhood, sometimes called the "Bloody 3rd" because of all the brawling that went on in the taverns and even the streets.

The children knew the reputation of the area where they lived, mostly because of Patrick Fahey, their father. He was standing outside waiting for them, next to a carriage that held two other adults. Patrick was the constable of the 3rd Ward, and he had broken up more than his fair share of bar fights amongst some of the more hot-headed Irish-Americans.

Patrick had come across the Atlantic Ocean from Ireland in 1841, immigrating to New York as so many Irish had done because of the terrible famine that had struck their island. His older brother Michael had purchased land outside of Milwaukee six years later, the Faheys being one of the original families to settle in Richfield, Wisconsin, in Washington County, which was just to the west of Milwaukee County. Patrick was 22 when he came to Wisconsin, and he joined his brother out at the homestead.

Patrick had met Mary Duffy, five years his junior. She was another Irish immigrant who had come to America through Toronto, Canada, then to New York, and finally to Wisconsin. Their courtship led to a wedding in 1849, and Mary Anne had been born the following year.

Farming was not what Patrick had in mind for a career, so in the mid-1850s he uprooted his family and moved to the 3rd Ward in Milwaukee and worked as a grader. That did not last long, and with the increase in violence and mounting tensions in the ward, soon he became a constable. At 35 years of age, he was slowly making connections within Milwaukee and was becoming involved in the politics of the city, as well as the nation itself.

Now, as he looked at his family piling out into the street, he smiled lovingly at his wife and kids. "Boys, are you ready to go with Uncle Michael and Aunt Mary for the weekend?"

"Aw, Dad, why can't we go on the boat to Chicago too? Mary Anne gets to go." William was not quite ready to give in.

"What's the matter, lad?" Michael bellowed out good-naturedly. "Are we not good enough for you?" He reached down and tousled the young boy's hair.

William blushed bright red. "No, Uncle Mike, it's not that. It's just how come Mary Anne gets to go? She gets to do everything, just 'cuz she's the oldest."

Uncle Mike glanced over at Mary Anne, who stood there grinning quietly. It was all he could do not to burst out laughing at the situation. He composed himself and then said, loudly enough for all to hear, "Ah, who wants to go to that dirty, smelly city when you can come out to the farm, enjoy the fresh air, have some fun with your cousins. It might even be warm enough to do a little swimming. After all, it is early September. What do ya say?"

Both William and Charles quickly lifted their heads at the prospect of swimming. They were all smiles as they clambered aboard the wagon behind the two adults. Michael winked at Mary Anne, and she returned the gesture. Looking down at his brother and sister-in-law, Michael called out to the boys, "Besides, I heard the teachers from school are going to be on the boat. Whoever heard of taking a cruise with your teacher? You should feel sorry for your sister."

Patrick nodded at the comment, and Mary mouthed a thank you to her brother-in-law for helping diffuse the situation. The boys were now content, and as they moved out into the street and headed out of town, Patrick turned to his wife and daughter and said, "Are we ready to head to the steamship dock?"

The steamship dock was actually the Dooley, Martin, Dousman and Company Dock, located about 5 or 6 blocks south and a block over at Erie and Water Streets. Mary Anne knew it would be just a short walk through the 3rd Ward to reach the dock…and the *Lady Elgin*. She could not suppress her excitement as she pranced around her parents. She had never been on a steamship, so this was a huge treat. She had overheard her parents say that each ticket cost one dollar. A whole dollar! She could barely believe that her parents would treat her to such an expensive trip.

"Yes, Daddy, we are all packed and ready to go, aren't we, Mommy?"

"Yes, dear, let's grab our bags and head on down."

Patrick decided to have a little fun with his exuberant daughter. "So how are you going to handle having some of the teachers on board as well?" His eyes twinkled as he waited for her reaction.

Mary Anne rolled her eyes. "It'll be fine, Daddy. I heard that it is a big ship, so I might not even have to see them."

Mary decided to chime in. "I heard that Mr. Connolly, Mr. Connoughty, and Mr. O'Mahoney are all going to be coming along. Is that right, Patrick?"

"I heard the same, and Mr. Rice, the school commissioner as well. Looks like you will have to behave yourself, Mary Anne?"

"Daddy, Mommy, stop!"

The Faheys burst out laughing. "Oh, Mary Anne, you know we are just teasing you," her mother chided.

"I know, I know, but it's embarrassing."

"Well, the good news is that a number of your classmates will be aboard, so you will have some friends to spend time with." Her mother had been in discussion with a number of families from the neighborhood, so she knew this to be true.

Patrick shook his head and commented, "I wonder if there is going to be anyone left here in town. Rumor has it that about 400 people are going. Should be quite the party. Well, let's head on down."

Down Milwaukee Street the trio sauntered, staying on the wooden sidewalk, and avoiding the muddy streets and carriages. "So what other kids my age are going?" Mary Anne asked her mother.

"Well, Eliza Wicks said she was going, and her daughter Eliza Jane and her little boy Nathan were going along as well."

Mary Anne knew that Eliza Jane was a year behind her at school, and Nathan was the same age as Charles. "Anyone else?"

"Emma Pengally. Isn't she in your class?"

"Yes, but I am not sure where she lives. She's new. Anyone else?"

Her mother hesitated a moment, which caused her husband to glance over at her. He saw a mischievous grin on her face. "Well, there are a couple of boys going along that you might know."

"Who might that be?" Mary Anne tried to sound uninterested, but there was a definite change in her tone when she asked.

"Oh, Willie Pomeroy, for one."

"Uh huh, anyone else?"

"Well, Captain Barry is bringing along his son William, too."

"Willie's going along?" Mary Anne's voice cracked slightly.

The Barrys lived just a block away on Jefferson Avenue, and the families knew each other well. The children all went to school together, which allowed Willie and Mary Anne frequent opportunities to see each other, a fact not lost on the Faheys.

"So is that a problem?" her father asked. He grinned over the top of his daughter at his wife, knowing that their daughter had developed a crush on Captain Garrett Barry's son, who was just a little more than a year older than her.

"No, no problem, Daddy," Mary Anne replied. And then she whispered to herself, "No problem at all."

Chapter 2

September 6, 1860

6:15 P.M.

Willie Barry stood at the steamboat dock, alongside his father, peering up and down the streets for any sign of familiar faces. He, too, was excited at the prospect of boarding the *Lady Elgin* for a weekend visit to Chicago. In addition, he was somewhat on his own for the next two days, as his mother and sisters were not accompanying the two of them. Being the only boy in the family, he was feeling a wave of freedom wash over him at the prospect of a "man's weekend." His father had good-naturedly teased Willie's sisters as the two of them had packed their belongings.

Willie's sisters had not been as upset as Mary Anne's brothers about missing an opportunity to visit Chicago. In fact, quite the opposite. "Good riddance," his sisters had commented, as he was double checking his bag. "A peaceful weekend without the 'men' around to ruin it."

Willie had just grinned and taken the ribbing with the spirit in which it was intended. He would never admit it publicly, but he loved his sisters a great deal, and would be the first to protect them should the need arise. Willie, like his father, did have a bit of the famous Irish temper, and he had been in a few fisticuffs already in his young life. His sisters knew unequivocally that their brother had their backs. Still, that would not stop them from chiding him constantly, to the point of torture.

"Oh-oh, a weekend away without Mommy watching over you," his oldest sister Johanna had teased. "The girls better watch out. Willie's on the loose."

The next oldest, Mary Ann, piled on, "Will your little friend, Mary Anne Fahey, be there? Maybe we better warn her that one Mr. William Barry might be calling on her."

Willie had turned beet red at that comment, and as his temper flared, his father cut the girls off. "Okay, you two that's enough." Garrett Barry had all he could to keep from laughing as well, but he knew that would only escalate the whole conversation. "Willie will be plenty busy helping me with Union Guard business in Chicago. It's unlikely he will have time for, uh, courting." He had grinned at his daughters with that last statement, and the girls burst out laughing.

"Da!" Willie had protested, but his father held up his hand, which put an immediate stop to the whole encounter. The girls, still giggling, gave their father a hug and said, "Love you, Da. You too, Willie." And off they had flounced to do whatever it was that teenage girls do. At last, Willie and his dad were left alone for their final preparations.

"How come Ma isn't here to say goodbye?"

Garrett Barry slowly rose from his chair, where he had finished polishing his boots, and looked thoughtfully at his son for a moment before answering. Willie noticed his dad's demeanor had changed with that question.

"She's taking care of some personal business, Willie. She told me to tell you she loves you, just in case she didn't make it back in time to say goodbye."

"What kind of business?"

"Personal!" Garrett Barry's tone was now taut with frustration. "That's all you need to know."

"Yes, Da," Willie had replied meekly. He knew when to stop pressing his father for information.

Still, even though his father could be intimidating, Willie still admired him. Without a doubt, Garrett Barry was his hero. Now, as he looked up at his father, standing there at the dock in his perfectly fit Union Guard uniform, he thought about all the stories he had heard about Captain Garrett Barry…and not just from family members, but people all over the 3rd Ward.

Garrett Barry had attended West Point, and his war record was commendable. He had served at Fort Snelling and Fort Crawford, had seen service in the Florida War, and probably the most well-known anecdote shared was his time spent in the Mexican-American War. He had fought bravely at the Battle of Monterrey in September of 1846.

He had fought alongside General Zachary Taylor as they defeated the Mexican army over the stretch of four days. Taylor was considered a hero for his actions both at Monterrey and later at the Battle of Buena Vista, where he and his men crushed Santa Anna. A year later, the Whig party had nominated Taylor to run for President. Despite having held no prior office, he defeated all comers and was sworn in as the 12th President of the United States in 1849. Unfortunately for Taylor, he took ill in July of 1850 and died in office before he was able to accomplish much.

Still, Willie could not help but admire his father even more. Not only had his father fought bravely for Willie's country, he had also personally known someone who had been the president. Willie shook his head when he realized that was not all Garrett Barry had accomplished.

Garrett had married and moved to Milwaukee, where his popularity increased. He became involved in politics, and the previous year he had been elected as Treasurer of Milwaukee County, as well as the superintendent of the post office. That was a feather in his cap, but it was nothing compared to what he was now embroiled in. As a matter-of-fact, the very trip that they were about to take was directly related to the uproar that was occurring not only in Milwaukee, but the rest of Wisconsin, and the nation as a whole.

Slavery. It was the word on everyone's lips, and Willie could scarcely be around a group of adults for more than a few minutes without the topic rearing its ugly head. Willie knew what his father thought of it. He despised the institution of slavery, as did most people living in Wisconsin. Willie had heard the word "abolitionist" tossed about in frequent conversations at the dinner table.

He had also heard of something called the "Underground Railroad." It was a system to help slaves escape from their masters in the South, which to Willie seemed like a good thing. He was not one that thought any group of people should be enslaved by another. Unfortunately for Willie, his father, and many of their highly emotional Irish neighbors of the 3rd Ward, slavery was legal. On top of that, there was another problem facing the abolitionists-The Fugitive Slave Act.

Ten years earlier, when Willie was only two, a law had been passed that allowed slave owners in the South to come to the North and physically take their slaves back. One of the problems was that these men would sometimes take free black men back South, not just escaped slaves. Black people had very few rights, and many judges in the North would simply look the other way when faced with the prospect of a trial involving whether a black person was a runaway or a free person. The slave owners would be able to return with their prize, and there was little anyone could do.

Willie knew his father was a law abiding citizen, a patriot through and through. He also knew Garrett Barry despised slavery, so it was very difficult for him to abide by a law that went against his convictions. This placed him in a quandary, particularly with the storm of protest that was occurring in Wisconsin. The leader of the state, Governor Randall, was an avowed abolitionist, as were many of the Republicans in office. So fanatical were some of them that there was another word that young Willie was hearing in adult conversation. Secession.

"Da," Willie looked up at his father, "can you explain secession to me?"

"Secession? What makes you bring up that horrible word?"

Willie paused, not wanting to say anything to get his father riled up. He knew that this topic was highly volatile, so he wanted to tread lightly. "Well, mostly I was trying to figure out why exactly we are taking this trip. I heard someone say it had something to do with secession, so really I want to know why we are making this trip. I thought it was about guns."

Garrett smiled grimly down at his son. "It's complicated, Willie. Tell you what, we have a lot of people coming with us to Chicago, so we need to make sure all is in order. I can talk to you a little bit on the way down to

Chicago if you'd like. For now, people are arriving and that steamer still isn't here. It was supposed to arrive by six, and it's already half an hour late. I hope Captain Wilson isn't having any trouble with the *Lady Elgin*. We are really counting on this excursion. Wouldn't want anything to go awry now, would we?"

"No, Da, we wouldn't," replied Willie.

"Besides, look, the Faheys are just arriving," Garrett grinned down at his son, who was blushing furiously.

"Da," came a whispered protest. "Knock it off!"

Garrett chortled, "I'm sorry, Willie. I know it's a touchy subject with you. I shouldn't tease you about it. Your sisters give you enough grief. Go say hello to them. Tell Mr. Fahey that I would like to speak to him, would you?

"Yes, Da. Be right back."

Willie scurried quickly through the gathering crowd toward the three Faheys. He felt very comfortable around the constable and his family. He and Mary Anne had been friends for quite a while, and there was a bond that had grown between them. Both families had seen it, which made it fodder for them to use on the two youngsters.

Fortunately, the rest of the world just saw a boy and girl who were simply friends.

Willie reached the Faheys and quickly relayed the message. "Good evening, Mr. and Mrs. Fahey. Uh, hi, Mary Anne. Mr. Fahey, my dad was wondering if you could go talk to him. Sounded kind of important."

Patrick Fahey grinned at young Willie. "Why, thank you for letting me know, lad. I'll head straight over. Mary, would you like to come with me, or do you want to chaperone these two?'

His wife could not suppress a smile. "Oh, Pat, stop. Go see Garrett. I see some of the other moms that are going down to Chicago. Mary Anne, why don't you and William go find some of your friends? It looks like the steamer isn't here yet, so we might have to wait a bit."

"Looks that way, doesn't it?" Patrick cut in. "Okay then, Mary, I will find you after I speak with Garrett. You two go have some fun. And behave." He gave his best glare at the two children. Both laughed nervously.

"Yes, Daddy," Mary Anne managed.

Garrett grinned, gave his wife a quick peck on the lips, and headed over to Captain Barry.

Mary let out a sigh. "Always teasing," she commented to Mary Anne and Willie. "Okay you two, go have fun, but make sure you are around when the boat comes in."

"Yes, Mommy, see you in a while." She gave her mother a quick squeeze and turned to Willie. "Well, where do you want to go?"

Her mother didn't wait around to hear the response. She started over to a group of mothers waiting nearer to where the steamer would dock, confident that young Mr. William Barry would keep her eldest child safe. "He's a good boy," she whispered to herself. "I'm glad they are friends. Lord knows what is in store for all of us."

Chapter 3

September 6, 1860

11:00 P.M.

"It's about time," growled Captain Barry. "We have been waiting for five hours."

"My apologies, Captain Barry. The delay could not be avoided. There was a bad bank of fog, amongst other things, that held us up." This was the voice of Captain John "Jack" Wilson. "We will head for Chicago as soon as we have everyone boarded."

Garrett Barry was not appeased. "What time will we be able to make Chicago? We have a number of events planned for tomorrow, beginning in the morning."

"Captain Barry, we will be in Chicago by dawn. The *Lady Elgin* will have no trouble making it there in good time. Of that I am sure." Captain Wilson spoke confidently.

Jack Wilson had every reason to be confident. He had been sailing the Great Lakes for years, and as captain of the *Lady Elgin* for over a year now, he was a well-known, competent, and good-natured sailor. He had an impeccable safety record, having never lost a single passenger in all his years of service.

His side wheel paddle steamer, the *P.S. Lady Elgin* was his pride and joy. She was one of the largest vessels on the Great Lakes, just over 250 feet long, and capable of holding over 1000 gross tons. The ship, while able to hold a great deal of cargo, was primarily a passenger ship, and this particular excursion was no exception. Somewhere between 300 and 400 Milwaukeeans were expected to make the 80 mile trip to Chicago.

Lady Elgin was ornately decorated, a showcase for luxurious travel on Lake Michigan and the other four inland seas that made up the Great Lakes. She was furnished with beautifully designed woodworking, and had more than 60 staterooms with approximately 200 berths for passengers to enjoy a good night's sleep aboard ship.

Garrett Barry inhaled deeply. He knew Captain Jack, as he was affectionately known, was a seasoned sailor, and was also providing a great service to all those that were presently boarding. Although the cost of one dollar per ticket was quite a sum for many of the working class Irish, Barry knew that it actually quite a deal that had been arranged between himself and the good captain.

"Okay, Jack. I know you would have been here earlier if there was anything you could have done about it. You know I am a bit on edge about all of the goings-on around here."

"I can imagine," Captain Jack replied. "Tell you what, Garrett, let's get these folks aboard, set out, and then why don't you stop up in the pilot house? Will your lovely wife and family be joining us?"

"No, just my son Willie is with me. The missus has 'business' to attend."

"I see," Captain Wilson commented slowly, stroking his bearded face. "Well, maybe you should bring Willie along with you, and I will make sure one of my mates gives him a proper tour of the ship while you and I chat. What do you say about that?"

"I think I will take you up on that offer, Captain. Thank you. I will come up once we are out of the harbor. For now, I should probably assist members of the Guard, especially with our prized possessions. Wouldn't want anything to happen to such a precious cargo, now would we?"

"Mm, hmm, I would whole heartedly agree," murmured Captain Jack.

Garrett walked down the gangplank to the shoreline, where a huge crowd was gathered, awaiting his instructions.

"Okay, everyone," he called loudly. "We are a bit behind schedule, as I am sure you are well aware." There was some raucous laughter at that statement. Garret waited until the volume had subsided, then continued. "The good captain has assured me that we will make Chicago by dawn, so let's help him out and proceed in an orderly fashion. Those of you who are families with berths, please board quickly, go to your cabins, and settle in for a few minutes so we can get the band, militias, and other goods and supplies on board as soon as possible. Once we have left port, please feel free to come up on deck, meet in the smoking lounge, or just call it an evening. Tomorrow is going to be a big day."

Captain Barry's orders were followed, and in short order, the excursionists were aboard, the City Band had boarded, and the militias- the German Black Yagers, the German Green Yagers, the Milwaukee Light Guard, and, of course, Barry's Irish Union Guard- quickly gathered together whatever cargo was left, including personal possessions. The gangplank was lifted, the whistle sounded, and the *Lady Elgin*, brightly lit up for all too see, left the dock on the Milwaukee River and headed out into Lake Michigan.

Meanwhile, Garrett Barry was searching out his son. Willie, who had spent the past few hours with Mary Anne, had boarded with the Faheys, and then had done what his father had commanded. He had gone to the stateroom that he would be sharing with his father, dropped off his belongings, and waited.

Garrett arrived just as Willie felt the boat begin to move. "Good, I see you found your way here," his father stated. "Let's head up on deck. The captain promised me that you could get a tour of the boat. Would you like that?"

Willie's eyes gleamed with anticipation. "Thanks, Da. That would be great!"

They exited their room and headed toward the pilot house. Garrett said, "I am sorry I have been so busy preparing for the trip. Did you have a good time with Mary Anne?"

Willie searched his father's eyes, looking for any sign of teasing. There was none. Relieved, he replied, "We had a good time just wandering around. Plus we ran into Willie Pomeroy, so the three of us just hung out together."

"Good. At least you were able to keep yourself entertained."

"Uh, Da."

"Yes?"

"Do you think the captain would mind if Mary Anne got a tour too?"

Garrett could not resist a grin. "You know what, Willie? I don't think he would mind at all. As a matter-of-fact, why don't we see if all the Faheys could join us?"

They did an about-face and headed back toward the staterooms. "Do you know which room is the Fahey's?" asked Garrett.

"Yes, Da. They are only two down from us. We all walked here together. That's how I know."

"Excellent." They were at the door momentarily. Garrett knocked on the door, and Mary Anne opened it. She smiled up at Garrett, and the smile became larger when she saw Willie just behind him.

"Good evening, Captain Barry."

"Good evening, Mary Anne. Willie and I were wondering if you and your mother and father would like to accompany us to the pilot house. The captain offered a tour of the ship, and Willie thought you might enjoy that."

Mary Anne turned excitedly toward her parents, who were approaching the door to join the conversation. "Ma, may we go? Please!"

Mary Fahey glanced at her husband, who shrugged. "I don't know Mary Anne. It's been a long day already, and it's late. Plus it will be a long day tomorrow," she replied.

"Oh, please, Ma. I really want to see the ship. And Captain Barry said it would be okay. Please!"

Patrick cut in. "It should be okay, Mary. We won't be too late. Plus the kids can come back to the boat any time tomorrow and rest if necessary."

Mary conceded "Fine, but I think I will call it a night. You two fathers can deal with your children if they are all grumpy tomorrow."

Patrick and Garrett grinned at Mary's response, and Garrett replied, "Well said, Mary. We will take responsibility for these two. It shouldn't be much more than an hour, I would guess. They should still have plenty of time to sleep before we arrive.

"Very well, but you two," she threatened, pointing at Patrick and Mary Anne, "better not wake me up when you come to bed." The twinkle in her eyes belied the threat, and both Patrick and Mary Anne gave her a quick, "Yes, ma'am," along with a hug from Mary Anne and a quick kiss on the cheek from Patrick.

"That's more like it," she responded. "Now get, before I change my mind."

Laughing, the foursome closed the door behind them and headed for the pilot house. Mary Anne asked right away, "Do we really get to see the whole ship, Captain Barry?"

"That's what Captain Jack said, and he is a man of his word."

They had reached the steps to the pilot house, and Garrett led the way up them and knocked on the door. Captain Wilson opened the door and noted that there were more people than had been invited originally. His raised eyebrows were met by Garrett's slight nod toward the first mate, who was at the wheel. Wilson nodded.

"Well, well, what have we here?" His voice was jovial, despite the surprise. "Looks like we have a couple of youngsters interested in a tour."

Garrett responded, "Yes, Captain Jack, this is Mary Anne Fahey, a friend of my son, Willie, here." He nodded down at Willie. "And this is Patrick Fahey, her father. Patrick is the constable in the 3rd Ward." The emphasis on the constable part did not go unnoticed by Captain Jack.

"Ah, well, it is a pleasure to meet you both." He shook hand with all of them, commenting to Patrick, "It's good to know we have the law on board, in case the partying gets out of hand. Of course, we have militia too, although they may be the ones we have to keep an eye on." He let out a bellowing laugh at his own joke.

Patrick, who had been slightly apprehensive, now relaxed and replied, "Well, let's hope none of that is needed. Thank you for allowing us the opportunity to see how the *Lady Elgin* operates. Isn't that right, Mary Anne?"

"Oh, yes, thank you so much, Captain! This is the first time I have been on a boat, and this one is huge!"

Captain Jack agreed, "That she is. That she is. I tell you what I am going to do. Since there are the two of you young people, I am going to have my First Mate here give you the royal tour. George, I can take the wheel, if you would be so kind as to show these two around." The captain turned back to the children. "To be honest, George is much better at giving tours than I am. Plus, Willie, I wanted to talk to your father about the rest of the weekend. Patrick, you are welcome to stay and talk with us, or you may take the tour as well."

Garrett promptly responded, "I think it would be a good idea for Patrick to join our conversation. Plus these two," nodding at his son and Mary Anne, "would probably prefer not to have adults around to ruin their fun."

"Agreed," Patrick replied quickly. "How does that sound, Mary Anne?"

With wide eyes, Mary Anne exchanged glances with Willie, and both of them shouted, "Yes!"

The adults burst out laughing. George surrendered the wheel to the captain, walked over to the pilot house door, opened it, and said jokingly to the two children, "They don't know what they're missing. It's a perfect night to roam around, both outside and down below. It will be my pleasure to escort you."

Willie and Mary Anne nearly bolted out the door, excited at their good fortune. A private tour of the *Lady Elgin* with the First Mate, and no parents supervising them! George, a wry grin on his face, nodded at the adults, closed the door behind them, and headed down the pilot house stairs to the deck below.

Chapter 4

September 7, 1860

12:00 A.M.

Almost as soon as the door closed, the mood became less light inside the pilot house. "So, Garrett, bring me up to speed on what has been happening lately," Captain Jack declared immediately.

Garrett took a deep breath, and both Patrick and the captain knew from past experience that this was a sign of great frustration and emotion. They were not disappointed. "Ah, that damn Governor Randall. I'm sure you know by now that he has relieved us of our rifles."

Captain Jack nodded, "Can he legally do that to you?"

Garrett replied, "Legally, yes, because even though the Union Guards are federal militia, they have been supplied by the state. The guns are the property of the state, but not our uniforms, which is why we still have those, at least. The guns are the reason we have sponsored this trip on your fine ship. The ticket price will more than offset the cost of the rifles we had delivered from St. Louis. We will reform as an independent militia that does not answer to the state, or that idiot in charge, Randall."

Patrick revealed even more information to the Captain. "Garrett fought Randall tooth and nail about this. Garrett has become increasingly strong politically, and that worries the Republicans. With Garrett's reputation as a soldier, and now that he is the County Treasurer in Milwaukee, there have been more than just a few whispers about him running for governor in the next election."

"Is that something you are interested in pursuing, Garrett?" Captain Jack queried.

Garrett confirmed the answer with a nod. "It's not just about being governor. I am not a power hungry politician. I just do not like where all this secession talk is heading. What they are suggesting is treason. I did not serve in two different wars, defending this Union, to watch my own state of Wisconsin secede if those fanatical Republicans don't get their abolitionist views answered immediately."

Captain Jack rubbed his slightly graying beard for a moment before responding. "Garrett, I appreciate your stance on protecting the Union, but you are an abolitionist yourself. Might I add, your wife might be even more ardent than yourself. You must really be conflicted about secession versus abolition of slavery."

The captain knew he hit a nerve with that statement. "Yes," Garrett acknowledged hotly, "Mary has ties with the Underground Railroad. I'm sure you figured out the reason she had 'business' tonight and isn't aboard was because she was down in Racine trying to help."

"Hmmm," Captain Jack avowed, "Must be difficult to want to preserve the Union while your own family breaks the Fugitive Slave Act, a federal law."

"My conscience does not allow me to follow a law that completely goes against my moral center. God forgive me, but I will continue to support my wife in her ventures." Garrett professed. "Besides, I wonder what cargo you might be hauling that caused you to be five hours late."

"Oh, you might be on to something there, Captain Barry. I am thinking that after this little excursion, I might take a little trip up toward Mackinac…and maybe Canada, if you get my drift." Captain Jack asserted.

"Oh, you have got to be kidding me?" Patrick cut in. "On board now?"

"No, no, I would never be so foolish as to do that and then bring 400 passengers on board. Too much chance of discovery. Our little delay in arriving was actually dropping them off at a safe house near, of all places, Racine. Looks like your wife is dealing with a few of my former passengers for a couple of days." He grinned. "I'll pick them up after we come back from Chicago. Constable Fahey, you are not going to have me arrested now, are you?"

Patrick smiled a bit grimly, "No, my wife is just as much against slavery as Garrett's, and I feel the same way. I would protect her with my life."

"Well, let's hope it doesn't come to that," the captain replied. He turned back toward Garrett. "Anything else I should know?"

"Not really. What is sad is that both sides here in Wisconsin want the same thing, abolition of slavery. Democrats and Republicans alike. It's just those damn Republicans want to secede. I wonder what their wonderful Mr. Lincoln would think of such a plan from some of his supporters. I know Douglas would never stand for it."

"Well, from what I have heard Lincoln say, his number one goal is to preserve the Union and uphold the Constitution. At least you and he agree on that point," proclaimed the captain.

"I suppose so," Garrett grudgingly admitted, "but I still think Douglas has the new immigrants' backs. The Republicans in Wisconsin are not fans of the Irish, Germans, or anyone else that has come across to America. That's why they confiscated our guns. We would not support secession, but I think it was more politically motivated than actual military strategy."

"Not to mention that he stripped you of your commission as Union Guard commander," added Patrick. "We were all upset about that, Garrett." Garrett Barry had taken control of the Unions Guards just two years earlier, and in short order had drilled them so thoroughly that they had become the pride of all of the militias in Wisconsin.

"Thanks, Patrick," Garrett responded, "I appreciate all of the Guards' support, as well as the Blacks and Greens from the German population."

Captain Jack rejoined, "Well, hopefully cooler heads will prevail, in Washington and in Wisconsin. Not so sure about in the South, though. Sounds like South Carolina is ready to secede if Lincoln is elected. They are afraid he will try to end slavery. What do some of your friends from the Mexican War say about that? Anything?"

Garrett thought about that question. "Well, Bobby Lee is from Virginia, and I know he had no problem arresting John Brown down at Harper's Ferry…or with the execution. Lee is all for the Union, but I think if push came to shove, he would protect Virginia first. The way he spoke about his state, a slave state, makes me wonder. Jackson, Longstreet, Beauregard, Sherman-all from the South. Some of our best military minds. Could you imagine if all of them helped the South secede and form their own country? Whoever becomes president would be bound by the Constitution to hold the Union together. That would mean war. God help us if that happens."

Quiet descended on the pilot house as each man wrestled with his own thoughts, his own actions. Should a man follow laws that conflict with his morality and personal beliefs? Each knew that supporting the Underground Railroad and ignoring the Fugitive Slave Act was just as much a crime as secession. Sometimes being a patriot wasn't as cut and dried as it appeared.

Finally, Captain Jack broke the silence. "So you got the guns though, eh?"

"Yes," Garrett replied, "We received a little help from a certain congressman who is sympathetic to our cause. 80 rifles at two dollars each. Government surplus muskets out of St. Louis, but they have been updated with percussion caps. Like I said before, that's why we are on board."

Patrick piped up, "You can even take a look at them if you like, Captain. We brought them along to show off in the parade tomorrow morning, or should I say this morning. Didn't even realize how late it has become."

Garrett concurred, "Maybe we should find those two children of ours before they drive your First Mate crazy." He gave Captain Jack a wry smile.

"Hmmph!" Captain Jack lamented. "If I know George Davis, he is probably planning a mutiny. He's probably recruiting your two youngsters as First and Second Mates and naming himself as Captain."

"Well, we can't have that, Captain," Patrick laughed. "It's not easy finding one as cooperative and competent as you."

"Haven't lost a soul yet," Captain Jack announced proudly. "And I don't plan on starting now. You two have a good night. I will see you in the morning. We will keep the *Lady Elgin* available throughout the day if some of your people need to take a breather. From the sound of the goings-on beneath us, I would say the party has most definitely started. Enjoy the trip, gentlemen."

"Thank you, Captain," the two Milwaukeeans chorused. Both men tipped their hats to the captain and exited the pilot house.

The captain turned his full attention back to steering the ship. He took a deep breath and muttered, "All right, Chicago, here we come. At least the weather is good."

Chapter 5

As Garrett and Patrick were leaving the pilot house, Mary Anne and Willie were just completing a cursory tour of the large passenger ship. George had been an excellent guide, just as the captain had promised. While he had not planned a mutiny with the two children, he certainly had won them over with his story telling.

"Ah, yes, she's a grand ship, she is," George had started right in as soon as they had reached the upper deck. "Do you know why she is called the *Lady Elgin*, per chance?" Both shook their heads no. "Well, she is named after the wife of Lord Elgin, who was the Governor General of Canada. You see, this here steamer was built in Buffalo just nine years ago, so if you do the math, Lord Elgin was still serving in that position when she was first launched."

"So then the *Lady Elgin* must be one of the newer ships on the water, shouldn't she?" Willie asked.

George rubbed his chin for a moment. "You would think so, but actually with the invention of other types of engines and whatnot, she actually is almost obsolete. Still, we wouldn't trade this old girl for some of that newfangled equipment. She has a grace and elegance about her that isn't found anywhere else on the lakes."

They were walking along the hurricane deck, and Mary Anne asked, "How much does a boat like this cost to make?"

"$95,000," was George's quick reply.

"Wow! And I thought a dollar for this trip was a lot," Mary Anne giggled.

George grinned at her naiveté. "Yes, it will take a good number of tickets to pay for her. That's for sure, but we also haul cargo in the hold and even bring the mail from one place to another. As a matter-of-fact, I believe we will have 40 head of cattle on here for the ride home."

"Really?" Willie whistled. "There must be a lot of room in the hold."

"Ah, that there is. We can take a looksee at that, and at the boilers if you like."

"That would be amazing, George. Yes, thank you," replied Mary Anne.

Willie agreed. "I would love to see how the ship operates."

"Well, let's head below decks then."

Down the three proceeded into the belly of the ship. First they were shown where supplies were kept for everyday use by the crew. George led them to the galley, where the crew cooked their meals. The he led them to the two boilers, which produced the steam that would power the massive ship's single cylinder, vertical walking beam engine.

"As you can see," George shouted over the noise in the boiler room, "we have to keep the fire stoked, so as to provide us with enough power to move such a large ship, and at a very fast speed. Of course, you probably saw the two giant smokestacks above decks where the exhaust from the fires leaves the ship."

"Are the boiler and engine the same age as the boat?" Willie asked.

"Now that's a great question, young man," George replied. "As a matter-of-fact, the rumor is no. I have heard that they came off a slave ship called the *Cleopatra*. Some sailors think that it was bad luck to have them installed on this ship."

"Why is that?" Mary Anne's eyes were wide with anticipation.

"Well, with all that has been happening in this country with arguments over slavery, and how so much pain and suffering was caused on the *Cleopatra*, it just seemed using them on a luxury ship such as this was just sticking salt in the wounds of all those slaves, so to speak. Still, that is a rumor. I am not sure if they are, in fact, from that other ship. Part of me says no, that it is just a story, but…" his voice trailed off.

Willie and Mary Anne pondered this unexpected piece of information for a few moments. Then Mary Anne asked the question that seemed to be hanging in the air. "So, has anything happened that would make you believe such a thing?"

George hesitated, not wanting to worry or upset his two young guests. Both of them saw a change in his demeanor, and that just peaked their curiosity. "It's okay, George. You can tell us," Willie said quickly.

George was none too sure about that, but looking at their expectant faces, he decided that little harm would come from sharing some of the *Lady Elgin's* history.

"Okay, but do not blame me if you have nightmares."

"Deal," Willie and Mary Anne chorused.

"All right, so after she was launched, the good *Lady* has had a series of misfortunes. First of all, six years ago she hit a reef near Manitowoc, Wisconsin and sank just as she reached the dock. No one lost their lives or anything, but she had to be raised and repaired, which took a while. Two years after that there was a fire on board, and some of the staterooms and the hurricane deck were damaged. Then two years ago, she was driven onto another reef in Copper Harbor, Michigan. They had to repair her again.

"How much does something like that cost?" Mary Anne wanted to know.

"I heard $8,000. That's a lot of money," George pronounced gravely.

"Is that all that has happened?" Willie wondered aloud. Both he and Mary Anne shivered, despite the warmth of the boilers.

"Not quite," the First Mate continued. "Just two months after getting repaired, she was stranded in Lake Superior at Au Sable Point Reef. More repairs were needed. Then last year major parts on the ship, the crossbeam and the crank pin broke on two separate occasions. So, as you can see, not the best of luck for this grand lady."

"Okay," Mary Anne spoke slowly, "but some of those kinds of things happen to other ships too, don't they."

"True," George responded, "but usually not that many to any one particular ship. But, hey, really, what could possibly happen between here and Chicago? It is one of the most traveled parts of the lakes. Shouldn't be any surprises this weekend."

The children thought about that comment and agreed that all of those events had reasonable explanations. They spent the next couple of minutes admiring all the mechanical parts that made up the entire boiler room, and then George suggested they start heading back up toward the main deck.

"Have you heard the story of the elephant?" George asked as they left the engine room.

Both of the children shook their heads. "Well, about six years ago," George explained, "this here ship had a very interesting cargo. It was a caravan of wild animals, including an elephant called Mr. Siam, leaving from Buffalo and coming to Milwaukee. Well apparently they had placed the elephant down below, and at some point along the way, when the captain wanted the wheelsman to avoid a perilous area, the wheelsman was unable to change course."

"What does the elephant have to do with it?" Mary Anne asked breathlessly.

George laughed, "Mr. Siam apparently decided that he would wrap his trunk around the steering chain and was in no mood to let go. His keeper finally managed to persuade Mr. Siam to release the chain. Good thing, too, or the *Lady Elgin* may have found herself run aground because of an elephant. How would a captain ever live that down?"

The children laughed at the thought of such a crazy thing occurring. Meanwhile, they had reached fresh air, George pointed out the paddle wheels. "This is a side wheel steamer. I'm guessing you are used to seeing the ships with the paddles on the rear of the ship, like they use on the Mississippi River. These side-wheelers are actually much more maneuverable because each paddle can be made to run in opposite directions, allowing the *Lady* to turn on a dime. Plus these paddles are each 32 feet tall. They can really push the water and give us speed."

"That really is something," Willie marveled.

"Mmm, hmm," murmured Mary Anne, "and look at the beautiful woodwork, and, oh, the staircase."

George smiled at the awe the children held for the mighty ship. "Yes, the grand staircase. She is elegant, isn't she? So much to do and see on the *Lady Elgin*. Of that, there is no doubt. There's even a smoking lounge for the gentleman and their cigars."

"Bet my dad would like that," Willie commented.

"Most definitely, he would. It tends to be a place where the men talk business, religion, politics, whatever happens to be on their minds, and kept away from their wives' ears, beggin' your pardon, Miss Mary Anne."

Mary Anne harrumphed at that statement, but she knew George was just telling it like it was.

"How do you like your cabins?" George asked.

"Oh, they are grand," Mary Anne gushed. "They are nicer than my room at home. That's for sure."

"We can hold about 200 people in those cabins, plus another 100 deck passengers, and we have a crew of about 40. Of course, it looks like the adults brought their own bartender, and it certainly sounds like the party has more than started."

It certainly had. They noticed some people enjoying the fresh air and other dozing off in order to be somewhat rested for a long day in the city. The band, however, had started playing, and a number of couples were dancing like there was no tomorrow. "Do you two want to join them, or continue the tour?"

Even in the light of the lanterns, George could see a flush of embarrassment on both sets of cheeks. When no response was forthcoming, he cracked a knowing smile and said, "Tour, it is." Both of the children breathed a sigh of relief.

"Now you can see those huge arches. Those aren't just for looks. They actually function to give support to the ship. Otherwise the torque from the paddles would rip themselves right off the ship. And, here we are, back to the pilot house. So, what did you think?"

"It was awesome!" Mary Anne's excitement flooded her features. "Thank you so much, George! You are a great story teller!"

"Yeah, thanks, George," Willie added. "This really is a great ship."

"Well, I'm happy that you enjoyed it, and look," he pointed at the stairway, where their fathers were just making their way down to the deck. "Perfect timing. Here you are Captain Barry, Constable Fahey, two children, safe and sound."

Both fathers shook his hand and thanked him for going above and beyond his duty.

"My pleasure, gentlemen. Now, I must see if the Captain needs me."

He ambled up the stairs, and after watching him go, Captain Barry gave a direct order, "Okay, you two, off to bed you go. Big day tomorrow."

"Yes, sir," they chorused.

"And don't forget that you are not to wake your mother," Patrick reminded Mary Anne.

"Yes, Daddy."

Chapter 6

September 7, 1860

7:00 A.M.

The beat of the drums and the melody of the horns from the City Band enveloped Mary Anne as she heard her mother's voice amongst the lively notes. "Mary Anne, wake up, child, or we will miss the parade."

Mary Anne salt bolt upright, remembering that she was not in her familiar bed at home, but aboard the large steamer, which was pulling into dock in Chicago. "Mommy, are we there yet? Have I missed anything else?"

"No, dear," her mother chided, "but that will not be true if you do not haul yourself out of that bed and get dressed quickly. Your father is already up on deck, and he is assisting the Guards in readying themselves to march."

Mary Anne was already pulling her dress over the top of her head as she concentrated on her mother's voice. "Why is it so difficult for girls to get dressed?" she complained. "I don't see the boys going through this kind of trouble. Sometimes I wish I could just pull on a pair of trousers and go." She had finally managed to fit her body into all the right holes in the dress, smoothed out some of the wrinkles, and was quickly smoothing out her hair. "Ugh! This is such a pain!"

Mary Fahey just grinned down at her daughter. "Guess we have a tomboy on our hands."

Mary Anne harrumphed at her mother's rejoinder. "Is that so bad? I could think of worse things to be."

"That's true," her mother confessed, "but for now the dress will have to do. Are you ready?"

Mary Anne glanced once more at her reflection in the elaborately framed mirror. With a shrug, she replied, "This is as good as it's going to get, I guess."

"It's very good, my darling daughter. You look lovely. Now, let's go up and find your father."

Mary Anne opened the door and stepped out, with her mother following and closing the door quietly behind her. Then they both headed in the direction from which the band was playing a lively Irish song.

They reached the deck as a beautiful sunrise met their eyes, and a warm wind blew on their faces. They strained to spy Patrick amongst the large crowd already on deck, even now becoming a bit rowdy and raucous. It was obvious that everyone was eager to explore the "Windy City," as it was already becoming known. Most had never been to this bustling city, despite it being a short boat or train ride away. Mary Anne was included in that particular group. Anticipation of what they would see and do was evident on their smiling faces and gestures toward shore.

The *Lady Elgin* was heading west, up the Chicago River, and as it reached a fork in the river where the two branches of the waterway flowed together, the wheelsman slowly turned the ship around to face the ever rising sun. In short order, he pulled the ship alongside the dock at LaSalle Street, to the cheers of the passengers lining her rails. The band continued to play, announcing to everyone that Captain Garrett Barry and the vaunted Union Guard had, indeed, arrived.

Mary Anne strained her eyes, both from the sun and her efforts to find a familiar face, her father's…or perhaps Willie Barry's. It was Patrick who found the two of them a moment later. "Good morning, my lovely ladies. Are we ready for a wonderful day in Chicago?"

"Oh, yes, Daddy. This is so exciting!" Mary Anne gushed. "What are we going to do first?"

"Well, Captain Barry said that some of the militias from Chicago are supposed to be here to greet us, and then we would parade through the city for a little bit before breakfast. From the looks of it, though, I don't see any of them here." He glanced at his wife Mary with pursed lips. "That will not make Garrett very happy, especially with the delay last night as well."

Patrick was correct in his assumption. Garrett Barry's ire was once again aroused. Being an extremely proud, as well as patriotic, man, he was feeling wholly slighted that the Union Guard had made this somewhat expensive journey, all for a good cause, and no one was available to receive them.

His two lieutenants, William Kennedy and John J. Crilley, along with the Milwaukee harbormaster, Martin Dooley, who was also an ensign in the Guard, stood alongside him. "Captain Barry, what shall you have us do? What are your orders?" Kennedy asked, as he stared at the nearly empty dock.

Barry observed the dock workers scurrying about to secure the ship to the moorings. The crew was readying the gangways, and the already anxious crowd gathered nearby, ready to disembark at the first word.

Garrett sighed, "I can't believe no one was here to welcome us. Well, never mind, we will greet these Chicagoans ourselves, in good Irish form. Gentlemen, as soon as our lively little group of partygoers is off this ship, gather the men, the new rifles, and the City Band. We will form our own parade."

"What route shall we take?" Crilley inquired.

"To the Merchant's Hotel for some breakfast. We will march up to the Court House, turn onto Jefferson, and make our way to State Street. The hotel is there on the corner. That route will allow our guests to see the Court House close up. It is an impressive building, even if it is in Chicago." His subordinates noted the smirk on his face and the jest in his voice as the name of the city passed his lips.

"Yes, sir!" they chorused. All bore huge grins at their captain's quip. Captain Barry was not going to let a little setback of no official greeting ruin this trip. Still, he would not forget it either, and his men knew that he would most definitely have a few choice words for the militia leaders that had left them abandoned at the dock.

The Guard's officers quickly passed along Barry's orders to the rest of the Union Guard, the two German Yagers' companies, and the Light Guard. The crew had already had the passengers disembark, so the militias were the only ones left aboard. Without delay, the men gathered their equipment, marched down the gangway, and onto the dock. There, they waited patiently for Captain Barry's orders.

Captain Barry was the last to leave the ship. He was giving orders to Willie and his friend, Willis Pomeroy. "You two," he said, "will follow behind us in the parade, making sure nothing is accidentally lost or left behind. You will also carry some of our supplies. Is that clear?"

"Yes, sir!" the two Willies chorused. Willie Barry was thrilled at the prospect of being a part of the militia's march through the large city of Chicago. That he had his lifelong buddy with him to share in it made it all the better. He was feeling more grown up by the minute. There was a slight twinge of disappointment that he could not spend time with Mary Anne, but as he and Willie P., as his father called his friend, gathered up some of the militia's belongings, it was soon forgotten in the anticipation of what lay ahead.

Chapter 7

September 7, 1860

9:00 A.M.

"Mommy, that courthouse was really big," Mary Anne stated, as the Faheys entered the Merchant's Hotel for breakfast. The family, along with most of the excursionists, and the Union Guard, had just finished parading through the streets of Chicago, and were now about to dine in one of the premier establishments in the downtown area.

"Yes, it was," Mary Fahey agreed. "What did you like best about it?"

"The dome on the top," was Mary Anne's instant reply.

"I thought as much," her mother laughed. "That is called a cupola, by the way, in case you are interested."

"That's a funny name. What is it for?"

Patrick, listening to the conversation as they waited to be seated, said, "Well, Mary Anne, in architecture it is used to allow in light and air, and for military use, it can be used as a lookout point. It's called a cupola because it resembles an upside down cup."

"What was that I heard about military use?" A familiar voice cut in to the family conversation. They all quickly looked behind them, finding Garrett Barry, Willie, and Willie P. just entering the hotel behind them.

"Captain Barry," Patrick responded, "we were just discussing the dome atop the courthouse. Would you three like to join us for breakfast?" He gave an almost imperceptible nod toward Mary Anne.

Garrett's eyes were sharp, and he caught the slight gesture from Patrick and grinned. "That would be wonderful, Patrick. What do you think, Willie? Shall we join the Faheys for breakfast?"

Willie caught the smile on his father's face, reddened slightly, but nodded quickly and said, "Sure, Da. Sounds good to me. I'm starving."

"Me, too," Willie P. chimed in.

The adults laughed at the response, and in short order the six were led to a table, where they were soon engaging in conversation about the day that lay ahead, in between bites of delicious pancakes, sausage, and assorted fruits and pastries.

"I grabbed the local paper during the parade," Patrick started in. "I see the Mechanic's Fair was judged yesterday over at the Wigwam. It's open for visitors to check out the new inventions that were best in show. Interested, Garrett?"

"In the inventions, yes. I'm guessing these two boys might like to see some of that newfangled machinery. Of course, it figures that they are holding it at the Wigwam." A somewhat loathing tone was obvious.

Mary sensed the disgust in his voice, and asked, "Is there something wrong with that location?"

Garrett apologized, "I'm sorry, Mary. It's just that Lincoln was nominated there back in May, and you know how I feel about the Republicans right about now."

Mary smiled slightly and replied, "That's okay, Garrett, I understand."

Patrick, listening to the rhetoric, responded, "I guess you should be glad we didn't come here yesterday then."

"Why is that?'

"Well," Patrick continued, "according to the paper there were about 2,000 Republicans marching through the streets, all boasting about Honest Abe and how he is going to save the country."

Garrett snorted, "Well, we will see about that. But you're right. It's a good thing we weren't here yesterday then. Some of our boys are a bit hot-tempered, to say the least. It would have taken quite a bit of restraint not to start a ruckus."

Mary Fahey, wanting to change the volatile conversation, especially with the children present, declared, "So, Patrick, what *else* was in the paper? Anything else we might want to see?"

Patrick caught the emphasis she had placed on her question, as did Garrett. They both grinned at her, letting her know that now was not the right time for what could become a very heated conversation.

"Ah, yes, what else?" Patrick rejoined. "Well, there is an Irish exhibition at Kingsbury Hall tonight. There is a huge canvas painting that shows the old homeland, along with some musical entertainment. That costs 25 cents to see. There's also a new theater that has a two part play, but that is 50 cents. A bit extravagant for us, but I am sure some of our guests will take it in."

Garrett nodded. "Anything else?"

Mary cut in. "Tell him what you told me is going on over by the Tremont House," she giggled.

Patrick smiled at his wife. "Yes, dear." He turned back toward Garrett. "There is a 'sale' on jewelry, silver, tableware, and cutlery across the way from Tremont House."

"Don't forget the diamonds," Mary added quickly.

"Yes, and diamonds," Patrick finished.

Willie, listening to the conversation, piped up, "Da, I think Ma likes diamonds, doesn't she?"

The Faheys burst out laughing, and Garrett shook his head at that comment. "Yes, Willie, your mother does like diamonds. I suppose we should probably stop in there to see what we might be able to bring back as a gift. After all, she stayed home with your sisters, and you were allowed to come along, so fair is fair. Plus, she is expecting again, so I would think that would make her happy as well."

"Congratulations, Garrett!" Mary beamed. "Another little Barry will soon be running around. I will have to stop over and see how Mary is doing when we get back to Milwaukee."

"I'm sure she would love that. Now, let's finish up eating so we can go enjoy the day. Plenty to do and see before tonight's political speeches."

The group soon finished the sumptuous meal, and before long were touring the city and enjoying the sights on a perfect late summer day. The warmth of the day filled their hearts with laughter, and the camaraderie of the group as they explored the city left no doubt that the future would be as bright as the golden sun above them.

Mary Anne, relishing this new adventure, commented to Willie as they perused the shops, "What a wonderful place! How lucky are we to have been able to come along!"

"I know," Willie responded, "my sisters are going to be so jealous when I tell them all that we did and saw."

Mary Anne giggled. "William and Charles Patrick were so jealous too. I suppose I will try to be a nice big sister and find some sort of souvenir for them. It's the least I can do."

Willie thought for a moment, and then shrugged. "I guess you're right. I should probably see if I can find something for my sisters as well, even if they do tease me all the time," he finished ruefully.

"I'll help you pick something out," Mary Anne offered. "I'm sure they will be excited for you to be back tomorrow."

Chapter 8

September 7, 1860

10:45 P.M.

Captain Jack Wilson wrinkled his nose as he sniffed the air on the hurricane deck of the *Lady Elgin*. It was not the familiar stench of the dock areas, nor the odor of the 40-50 head of cattle that had been brought aboard and penned on the main deck in somewhat rickety enclosures, or even some of the passengers who reeked of alcohol, that brought the grimace to the good captain's normally tranquil appearance.

He sighed, and then turned to Captain Barry, who was standing alongside him, watching some of the more exuberant passengers stumble onto the ship. "There's a storm coming, Garrett, a big one, unless I miss my guess. Considering the ship is a bit overcrowded, especially with the cattle on board, I feel it is prudent to hold off on returning to Milwaukee tonight."

Garrett Barry was in no mood to argue with Captain Jack. He was frustrated by the events of the day, and try as he might to remain calm, he burst out, "Dammit, Captain, these people have no place to stay for the night. No arrangements were made for us to stay here in the city. You have these stinking cattle on board that need to get to Milwaukee, and the mail needs to be delivered as well. We need to leave now!"

Captain Jack stared at Captain Barry. "What has you so worked up, Garrett, that you would risk life and limb to get home?"

"This whole day has been full of problems. First, no one was here to greet us. Then, Douglas wasn't even here to give a speech. Next, no mention of the reason for our visit was even mentioned at the rally. And now I have to deal with a bunch of drunken Irish fools coming aboard. We just need to get these people home and be done with it."

"Garrett, I understand your frustration, but with the weather that is coming in, it is just a bad idea to head out right now."

Garrett was not to be reasoned with. "Captain Wilson, did we not charter your boat for this excursion? We would like to be on our way home. Isn't that right, boys?" he called out to a number of Union Guardsmen waiting nearby.

A roar arose from the men gathered there, and Garrett, now invigorated by the support of his men, continued, "Aren't you Captain Jack Wilson, the one who has never lost a soul on his watch, the one who has been called the greatest captain on the Great Lakes? Are you afraid of a little storm?"

That little jab at Captain Jack hit the mark. Captain Jack was not foolhardy, was not one to take chances with crew, passengers, and cargo, and had indeed sailed in very rough weather numerous times without incident. He was good-natured and kind, but even he had his limitations. Garret's statement angered him, and for the first time on this weekend trip, everyone received a glimpse of what lay beneath the cool, calm exterior.

"All right, listen up!" Captain Jack bellowed, so loud that Garrett actually took two steps backward at the volume and force of his voice. "It is 11:03 right now. We are leaving this dock at 11:33, one half-hour from now. If you are on this ship at that time, and you do not belong, then you will be accompanying us to Milwaukee, and you will have to find your own way back. If you know of someone who is supposed to be on board and has yet to return, you had better find them now! Otherwise we leave them behind."

The intensity and poignancy of his announcement left all within earshot stunned momentarily. It was eerily silent on deck for a few moments. Then there were some murmurs, and finally people began to move about. Some who had imbibed a bit too much were assisted to their staterooms to sleep it off. Others began grabbing their possessions and hurrying to their rooms or to one of the lounges. Captain Wilson stomped to the stairs that led to the pilot house, climbed them, and then disappeared inside, apparently to cool down.

The Faheys, along with Willie and Willie P., had been on the edge of the conversation between the two captains. The alarming manner in which Captain Jack had addressed the crowd, and then exited, left them completely dumbfounded. Even Garrett, who now walked over to them, was somewhat shocked.

He looked remorsefully at his son. "I may have gone too far with that last comment. I better let Captain Jack settle down and then go apologize to him. What I said was uncalled for. Insulting someone's manhood is never a good idea, Willie, especially someone who is as good a man as Captain Jack."

Willie nodded. He was taken aback by the whole encounter, knowing his father to be a hard, just man, but not insulting. Then to hear him saying he was wrong and needed to apologize. Well, Willie could not think of many times his father had been wrong, let alone apologize for it. Only Willie's mother had that kind of power over Garrett Barry.

Mary Anne was also staring wide-eyed at Garrett, almost in disbelief. She knew that her father, too, had moments where his Irish temper got the best of him, but, like Willie, she knew the only person Patrick Fahey would apologize to would be one Mary Fahey. To see and hear that statement from someone as famed as Captain Garrett Barry, only deepened their admiration for the man.

Patrick was the first to speak. "Captain Jack doesn't hold grudges, Garrett. What do you say about getting these kids to bed? It's late. Once they are down for the night, we can buy him a drink. I think he understands your frustration." Patrick glanced at his wife, who nodded her assent.

Garrett took a deep breath. "That sounds like a good idea. Okay, Willie, it has been a long day. Let's go to our room, so you can get some sleep. Patrick, I will stop by to grab you on the way to see the captain. A drink might do us all good. Say good night, Willie."

"Good night, Mr. and Mrs. Fahey. Good night, Mary Anne. See you in the morning."

"Good night, Willie," the two adults replied.

"See you in the morning, Willie," Mary Anne whispered softly.

As they settled in for the night in their stateroom, Mary Anne asked her father, "Daddy, is it safe to sail back to Milwaukee? Captain Jack was worried about the weather. Is there a problem?"

"Don't worry, Mary Anne, Willie's dad was right about one thing. Captain Jack is the best sailor on the Great Lakes. Maybe he shouldn't have said what he said, but Captain Barry trusts the captain implicitly. If there was certain danger, Captain Jack would not have left port. Storms happen, and the waves might make for a little bit of a rough ride, but this is a fine ship, with a fine captain and crew. I can't think of another ship I would rather be on than this one. Now, you need to try and go to sleep. Otherwise, you will be all grumpy when we reach Milwaukee." Patrick smiled down at his daughter as she snuggled under her blankets.

"Yes, Daddy. I love you."

"Love you, too," Patrick replied. "See you in the morning." There was a soft tapping on the door. "That will be Captain Barry. I'll tag along with him to see the captain." He turned to his wife. "I will be back shortly. Don't wait up for me." Mary nodded.

Mary Anne waited until her father left the room, and then said quietly to her mother, "Mommy, I'm a little afraid."

"Of what?"

"Well, Willie and I learned some things about the ship we are on, and some people think the *Lady Elgin* is cursed."

Mary stared at her daughter, trying to suppress a laugh at such an idea as a curse, but when she saw that her daughter was actually frightened, she immediately sat down beside her on the bed and began to stroke her hair reassuringly. Ever since Mary Anne was a little girl, her mother knew this would comfort her. In a few moments,

Mary Anne began to relax. Her mother cooed softly, "Everything will be fine, Mary Anne. Like your father said, we have the best captain around. Now close your eyes. I will stay with you until your father comes back."

Mary Anne closed her eyes, and in a few minutes, with the music from the lounge above her floating down into the cabin, and the waves gently rocking the ship, she fell asleep.

* * * *

Unbeknownst to Mary Anne and all those aboard the *Lady Elgin* as she pulled away from the dock in Chicago, a schooner named the *Augusta of Oswego* was slowly making its way south on Lake Michigan. If Mary Anne thought that the *Lady Elgin* might be cursed, a conversation with the captain of the *Augusta* would have certainly given her nightmares.

26 year old Captain Darius Malott had guided his ship past the lights of Milwaukee earlier that evening, and he was rejoicing that they would soon be pulling into Chicago with a huge load of lumber. This late in the season, he was anxious to deliver his cargo and return to his wife of only three years.

The *Augusta* was a new ship for the captain. He had only been put in charge of the sailing schooner the month before, so he was learning how she handled as he went along. He noted that laden with such a heavy load of lumber, including a full load in the hold, as well as more stacked high on the deck, the *Augusta* was not the easiest ship to maneuver. Quite the opposite, in fact. She did not respond quickly when trying to change course, and this left Malott with an uneasy feeling in the pit of his stomach.

Thoughts drifted back to other unfortunate events that seemed to follow him no matter where he sailed. It has all started back when he was about 18, and he was working as a dockhand. He and his uncle had been helping load cargo onto a ship when a fight broke out between his uncle and a deckhand on the ship. When young Darius came to his uncle's defense, he had broken the deckhand's arm as well as his leg.

This left the crew one man short, and since Darius felt responsible, he signed on to the ship named the *Ellen Park*. So began his sailing career, but unfortunately for him, it would be a career plagued with disaster. Darius would transfer to other ships, and on one, the *Gold Hunter*, an event occurred that still made him sick to his stomach.

The ship was heading to England when a storm took down the mast and swept the captain and first mate overboard. Stranded in the ocean, with no way to sail, the crew's supplies began to dwindle. Finally, after nearly seven weeks on the ocean, with nothing left to eat, it was decided that someone needed to be sacrificed and eaten so that the others could survive. Only two, Darius and his friend George Dormer, were unmarried, so the rest of the crew decided that they should die first. Drawing straws, George lost, and the crew killed him and began to eat him. It was only then that another ship passed nearby and rescued them.

Malott shivered in the Lake Michigan evening as he recalled the incident, thanking God that he had not been next on the menu. Still, bad luck continued to follow him. After he reached England, he would take a job as second mate on another ship, and as they were sailing in the Pacific Ocean, they ran into terrible weather, forcing people to stay below deck. With poor ventilation, a number of them suffocated. If that were not enough, then the ship caught fire, and Darius, along with some of the other crew members, were left drifting for 32 days until they finally reached South America.

After those episodes, he decided to stay closer to home, and began sailing on the Great Lakes. He would meet his future wife, Mary, and they would make a home near Point Pelee, along the Canadian shore on Lake Erie. Darius smiled as he reminisced about his stop at his home just before he had headed the *Augusta* through Lake Erie, into the Detroit River, and then into Lake Huron, with a stop at Port Huron, Michigan, to pick up his current load of lumber.

The smile faded as a lightning bolt illuminated the huge thunderheads that had formed quickly in the night sky. The wind began to whip around from the northeast. Sailing in a nor'easter in the Great lakes was a frightening prospect for even the most seasoned sailor. Malott swore, "Dammit, we are so close." A sense of impending doom closed in on him. He called to his second mate, George Budge, to handle the wheel for the time being. Darius then went below deck to check on the cargo and to make sure that everything was lashed down securely.

By the time he finished, it was about 2:00 a.m. on September 8, 1860. As the storm increased and waves began to pound the 128 foot long schooner, Malott heard the voice of his second mate calling for him to come topside. He, along with the first mate, John Vorce, hurried up the ladder, only to find that the sails were still up. Malott quickly ordered the sails to be taken down, but as his orders were being followed, a huge gust of wind, along with ever heightening waves rolled the ship, caused the lumber on the deck to shift. The *Augusta* listed sharply.

Through the pouring rain, George Budge spotted lights over the bow of the ship. "Captain, look!"

Malott hurried toward the prow of the ship to see what the problem was. There, not even a quarter of a mile away, were the bright, red lights of a steamship, crossing in front of the *Augusta*. "Hard up!" Malott screamed, but it was too late. The *Augusta*, already difficult to manage, would not respond to the helm. Malott looked on helplessly as his ship, at nearly a right angle to the passing steamer, tore into the left side of the *Lady Elgin*, just forward of the paddle wheel.

Malott heard and felt the sickening crunch, and was nearly thrown to the deck. As he righted himself, he thought, "Not again."

Chapter 9

Mary Anne was jolted awake by a loud crashing sound and a force that threw her off the bed and onto the floor. Her mother and father were also awake, listening to the sounds of the storm raging outside. The jolt had awakened them as well, but fortunately for them, they had not been dislodged from their bed. Her mother rushed over to her and asked anxiously, "Are you okay, honey?"

Mary Anne shook the cobwebs out of her head. "I'm fine," she replied, checking herself over to make sure nothing was broken or bleeding. "What happened?"

"I'm not sure," Patrick responded. "I think I will go have a quick look." He began pulling on his clothes rapidly. He was just reaching for the door when there was a knock. He turned to look at his wife and daughter with a look of apprehension. Mary Anne had seldom seen her father's expression so alarmed. "Who could that possibly be?" he wondered aloud.

Opening the door, he found Garrett and Willie, hair in disarray, half-dressed, and with the same troubled expressions on their faces. "Get the women dressed now, Patrick," he ordered. "Quickly, and get them up on the hurricane deck. There's been a collision. A schooner hit us right by the paddlewheel, and there is a lot of damage to the ship. We are taking on water. Hurry!"

Both Mary Anne and her mother gasped at the news, and Mary Anne needed only one look at Willie's face to realize that he was thinking the same thing. *Was the Lady Elgin really cursed?* Both jumped up immediately, however, and in moments were dressed well enough to leave the room and head to the upper deck and into the heart of a storm.

In the hall, the group ran into the Eviston clan, which included couples John and Ellen, Thomas and Bridget, and their single brother, Martin. What Mary Anne heard next seared into her mind. "We are in a terrible fix," Thomas was saying to the rest of his group. "I was down looking at the hole in the steamer, and you could drive a team of horses through it."

Mary Anne had no time to listen to any more of the conversation, as her parents pulled her along the hallway.

Farther on they ran into Tim O'Brien, who was telling his wife, daughter, and others from his group to stay put and he would return for them. Mary Anne's parents continued up the stairwell, finally arriving at the upper deck. In moments they were completely soaked as torrential rain came pouring down on their heads, and hurricane force winds whipped and pulled at them, threatening to send them sailing off the ship and into the dark turbulent waters below.

They were directed by crewmen to go to the starboard side of the ship. Mary Anne noted that the cattle seemed to have disappeared. She was puzzled by their disappearance, until a flash of lightning illuminated the water, and she saw the cows' futile attempts to swim in the large waves. They had been driven off the ship in order to lighten it, and shortly thereafter they had all drowned.

As she huddled by her parents in the raging storm, Garrett and Willie made their way over to the Faheys. "Willie, stay here with Mary Anne and her mother. Patrick, help me get some life preservers for them." Patrick and Garrett disappeared in the ever growing crowd on the hurricane deck.

"Life preservers? Why do we need them? Are we sinking?" Mary Anne's voice shook in fear. She grabbed Willie's hand. He squeezed it to try to comfort her, but a lightning flash showed the fear in his eyes as well. Suddenly Willie P. appeared next to them, gasping as if he had just run a marathon.

"There's a big hole in the ship," he cried out. "They are trying to plug it with mattresses, but it's not working. I heard them say that the boat is sinking."

There were banging and chopping noises heard over the fury of the storm. "What is happening?" Mary Anne asked Willie P., hoping he could provide some sort of sense to this insane event.

"The firemen are trying to chop the hurricane deck free so people will have something to hang onto. I don't think there are enough life preservers for everyone." That revelation frightened Mary Anne even more, if that was possible. She clenched her fists, closed her eyes, and silently begged, "Please let this be a bad dream. Please let me wake up. Please!"

Her pleas went unheard, and moments later they were all jolted sideways as a monstrous wave smashed into the already badly listing ship. Mary Anne opened her eyes just in time to hear snapping metal and watch the smokestacks tear loose from their iron support rods. She watched helplessly as, almost as if in slow motion, the stacks began to fall toward the deck below. To the horror of Mary Anne, and everyone around her, the smokestacks came crashing down directly on top of a group of women who were in the path, crushing them to death instantly.

Screams and curses echoed through the night, a cacophony of agony and despair. Mary Anne looked around her to see who else she might recognize. She found that the majority of the people gathered together were women and children, including a number of infants and very small children. A nauseating feeling swept over her as she realized that there was no way those little ones could swim. If the ship did sink…Mary Anne shook her head, trying to clear her mind for what she now realized was about to occur.

Patrick and Garrett had made their way back to the other four. The strain on their faces revealed the truth. The *Lady Elgin* was not going to make it to land. Still, Garrett Barry was not going to panic. He had fought in battles with enemy bullets whistling by. He was not about to succumb to fear now. "Now listen, all of you! We are going to do everything we can to survive this. Hear that bell?" Over the roar of the storm, the wailing sound of the ship's bell called out for assistance. "The schooner that ran into us can hear that bell, so they know to stand by and help when the ship sinks."

Mary Anne and both of the boys locked eyes. *When, not if.* Garrett knew what this news was doing to them, so he tried to encourage them. "If we all stick together, and help each other, then we will get through this. Do everything you can to stay together."

Waves continued to crash into, and onto, the *Lady Elgin*, as she sank lower in the water. The storm continued to pound the people waiting helplessly on the hurricane deck. The chopping and pounding by the firemen continued. Shrieks and cries for help were constant.

Without warning, another large wave washed over one end of the hurricane deck, and before Mary Anne's eyes a small group of men, women, and children were swept into the open water. Flashes of lightning showed heads bobbing, reaching for anything that might sustain them and keep them afloat. Between flashes, Mary Anne strained her eyes to see who might be still floating in the water. The number of heads declined with every burst of light from the sky. Mary Anne began to sob, and her mother held her close. Both waited for the next wave to take them to their death. Mary Anne looked over at her friend Willie, who was being held by his father, and saw that he, too, now feared the worst.

Suddenly a grating, grinding sound of splintering of wood met their ears. The hurricane deck, which had been partially cut loose by the firemen, tore away from the remaining supports, popped up in the water, and started floating away from the doomed ship. Mary Anne and Willie stared in disbelief. They were on an oversized raft with over a hundred other people, hanging on literally for dear life. Some who had been tossed into the raging waters, struggled to reach the now life preserving deck. Others looked for anything else that might be floating by, pieces of wood, life preserver planks, musical instruments, and even carcasses of dead cows.

Soaked as she was, Mary Anne was not as cold as she thought she would be. Because it was early September the Lake Michigan water was still warm enough so that hypothermia would not be an issue. In fact, the air was actually colder, so she soon realized that being partially submerged actually made her feel warmer. Others were coming to the same conclusion, and as they floated on the makeshift raft, they would dip parts of their body into the water to remain warm.

As the group on the hurricane deck watched, the *Lady Elgin's* engine tore loose from the bolts that held it in place, falling over and ripping another hole in the ship. The ship moaned and groaned as it began its final descent into the dark waters of Lake Michigan. One more gigantic wave crashed down on the ship, and it first split in two, and then splintered into hundreds of pieces. The scene reminded Mary Anne of a box of oversized matchsticks extending out and away from those stranded on the floating deck. Moments later, what was left of the ship slipped beneath the waves. The *Lady Elgin* was gone.

Chapter 10

September 8, 1860

3:00 A.M.

As the lightning flashed, the thunder boomed, and the waves pounded at the makeshift raft that was the hurricane deck, Captain Wilson bellowed out to all those still aboard or struggling to hold on.

"Everyone! Quiet! Do not move unless you absolutely have to. We need to keep as still as possible. We don't know how stable or strong this raft is, or how long it will hold together in these waves. Do everything you can to help one another, but try to remain calm and motionless."

There was a quiet consent amongst the hundred or so persons aboard the large, wooden structure that had once graced the upper level of the *Lady Elgin*. Captain Wilson somehow was able to move between the huddled masses, shouting words of encouragement, as well as any suggestions he thought might help the passengers, particularly though who had been injured when the ship went down.

Mary Anne, shivering from the exposure to the storm, asked her father, "Where is the other boat that ran into us, Daddy? I thought they were going to help us."

Patrick shook his head. "I don't know, Mary Anne. I don't know. I can't believe they would have just left us here to…" He didn't finish the sentence. There was a pause, and then he continued, "How did this happen?"

Another man, John Jervis, also from Milwaukee, was hunkered down with his wife, Margaret, alongside the Faheys and Barrys. He spoke up, "I saw the whole thing. I was up on deck, right in front of the one paddle wheel, and saw a light on the water. It was closing on us fast, and when I realized that there was going to be a collision, I ducked out of the way. That other ship, a sailing schooner hit us square, right in front of the wheel. It smashed right through the walls, and the front part of that ship broke off in the main cabin."

"A sailing schooner?" Garrett asked.

"Yes, and it still had some of its sails up. In this weather, what could they have been thinking? Not only that, it was listing quite a bit, so something may have been wrong aboard her as well. Still, I can't believe they would have left without checking to see if we were damaged."

"Then what happened?" asked Patrick.

"First, the crew tried to stem the flow of water by plugging it with mattresses. That didn't work, and the water put the fire out in the boilers, so the ship could not move. Then Captain Wilson ordered the lifeboats lowered to try to patch the hole from outside, but I think the rowboat only had one oar because I heard them yelling to throw down an oar. Most of the crew was on that rowboat, and it drifted away. A few more crewmen lowered a second boat, but it swamped, and they were unable to help us either. They were able to right it, and I think about 8 or so were on that one. They drifted away too, just before the ship split apart and sank."

Mary Anne, huddled with her mother and father for warmth, took in the explanation, but it did little to remove any fear she felt inside. She peered through the darkness, searching in the blackness for Willie's face. When another round of lightning brightened the sky above them, she saw the look of dread in his eyes too. Were they going to die out here, just a few miles from shore?

The storm continued to rage on. Waves pounded the raft, and each time it seemed less people were left aboard, and the raft appeared to be shrinking in size. The weakened deck was being slowly splintered apart, taking with it two or three people at a time on very small pieces of decking, or sometimes just washing them off completely, leaving them struggling alone in the water, screaming for help, and then...silence.

Mary Anne squeezed her eyes shut, trying to blot out the sights and sounds of the horror around her. She would open them again, only to find that this was indeed happening, and it was not a nightmare, but a terrifying reality. She looked to any individual whom might save the day, and it was then she saw a feat of heroism that gave her hope.

John Crilley, one of the Guardsmen who had himself just crawled on board the raft with some assistance from Captain Jack, saw a woman struggling in the water. He reached out, grabbed on to her by her hair, and yanked her aboard. To his and everyone else's disbelief, the woman, Johanna Rice, the school commissioner's wife, was clinging to a baby. Even more amazing, the baby was still alive!

Once she was aboard, Johanna delivered the infant to another woman, Ann Kennedy, who was the child's actual mother. Johanna had risked her life to save the baby, even though at that moment, her own husband and son were missing.

Captain Jack was near Mary Anne when she heard another man say to him, "I don't see how that child can possibly survive."

Captain Jack's response lifted Mary Anne's hopes even further. "Whoever may be lost, she must be saved." The determination in his voice buoyed Mary Anne's spirits, even as the raft continued to struggle to remain in one piece and afloat. Mary Anne moved slightly, so she could be nearer Willie.

"I think we can make it, Willie. Captain Jack, just look at him. He's going to find a way to get us to shore. Somehow." Despite the hope in her heart, there was still doubt in that last word.

Willie, appearing to be a bit dazed and confused, mumbled, "I hope so, Mary Anne. I hope you're right."

Mary Anne looked up at Willie's father. "What's wrong with Willie, Captain Barry? He doesn't sound right?"

Garrett Barry, tending to his son, shook his head. "When we took that plunge into the water, I think something hit him in the back of the head. He has some head injuries. I think it best if we try not to talk too much, Mary Anne."

By the strained tone of his voice, Mary Anne knew that something was dreadfully wrong. She nodded, unseen in the darkness by Captain Barry, but then asked, "Would it be okay if I stay by him?"

Garrett Barry, a man who had seen the gruesomeness of war, was at the moment in dismay for the health and well-being of his battered and bruised son. That this little girl was somehow remaining calm and offering assistance almost overwhelmed him. "Thank you, Mary Anne. Yes, please sit by him and try to keep him as still as you can. He's hurt pretty badly."

Mary Anne placed an arm around her friend. Willie Pomeroy was snugged up against him on the opposite side.

He spoke across his friend to Mary Anne. "We'll get him home, the two of us, won't we, Mary Anne?"

"That's right, Willie P., all of us are going to make it home."

Chapter 11

September 8, 1860

4:00 A.M.

Another hour had passed. The storm had not abated, and the hurricane deck was disintegrating with every passing wave. Mary Anne was becoming more and more frightened with each passing moment. What if a wave broke off the piece of the raft that she was on? What would happen if a wave washed her off? She was not very good at swimming, and with her dress on… and the storm…and the large waves…

"Mommy, I'm afraid of the water," she said aloud.

Mary Fahey, still trying to fathom how this catastrophic event could have occurred, was wrestling with not only her own survival, but that of her 10 year-old daughter, as well as wondering what would become of her two boys if the worst should happen. She was as frightened as any of the rest on that raft, but she spoke to her daughter as calmly as if they were on an afternoon walk in the Third Ward.

"I know, Mary Anne, but we have Captain Jack, and Captain Barry, and your father all with us. If anyone can handle this, those three can. Just try to hang on for a little longer. We are floating toward shore. It will be light soon. Hopefully the storm will finally end, and then someone will find us."

As if mocking Mary's words, Mother Nature decided at that moment to send a monstrous wave over the top of the raft. It crashed down, splintering the raft into four large pieces. Screams filled the night as the survivors struggled against the storm, the blackness, the water.

Mary Anne had moved slightly to her left to speak with her mother, who was sitting next to her husband. Patrick had his arms locked around his wife when the wave hit. The place where Mary Anne had been sitting, next to Willie, disappeared as the raft tore apart. Had she not moved, Mary Anne would have been swept into the broiling waters. As it was, she found herself dangling on the very edge of the small piece of raft that now contained just her and her parents. Patrick, in pure panic, clutched at Mary Anne and pulled her on top of him and her mother.

"Willie!" Mary Anne screamed. She craned her neck to find her friend, but in the darkness, it was to no avail. Finally another bolt of lightning split the sky, and the Faheys were able to distinguish the large part of the raft that still held the Barrys, Willie P, the Jervises and Captain Jack. Mary Anne began sobbing; both from the predicament they were in now, and also because she had been separated from her friends, who were still afloat on another piece of the deck.

Mary pulled her close and squeezed her tight, as if she were an infant rather than a 10 year old. Patrick contemplated the situation his family was now forced to endure. With just the three of them, it was going to be extremely difficult to survive without any help. He watched as the waves sped the larger raft away from them. Soon it became difficult to see the others at all. With a change in the wind, now coming from the northeast and pushing them in a more southerly direction, it was not long before they were lost from sight.

Meanwhile, on the other raft, Willie was conscious, and cognizant of the fact that his friend was no longer sitting beside him. He shrieked, "Mary Anne!" The pain from his wounds overcame him, and he slumped back down next to Willie P. His father, recovering from the shock of the wave and the fact that his friends were no longer beside them, quickly came to his son's side.

"Willie, can you hear me?" he shouted over the reverberation of the thunder. No response.

Garrett took hold of his son and held him close, listening intently for breathing. There was a weak, raspy exhalation from Willie. He was barely conscious, and with all that Willie had been through, Garrett was now troubled that the head injury that his son had sustained might be even worse than he first had suspected.

"Is Willie going to be okay?" Willie P. asked, tormented that his long time friend's life might now be in more danger than just being afloat on a stormy lake following a shipwreck.

"It doesn't look good, William," Garrett replied.

Captain Barry almost never used his given name, so Willie P. realized the direness of the situation. He had already seen Mary Anne disappear into the waves, and the thought of losing another friend was beyond comprehension. He latched on to Willie, looked up at Captain Barry, and with great determination stated, "I won't let anything happen to him, Captain Barry. If you get us to shore, I will make sure Willie gets there with us."

Had the situation not been so ominous, Garrett might have smiled at the young man's pledge to protect his best friend. Instead, he grasped Willie P.'s shoulder and simply stated, "Thank you. You are a good friend. Let's hope Captain Jack has an idea or two. I'm good on land, but this is his arena. I am going to try and make my way over to him and see what else we can do."

As it turned out, it appeared to be a fortuitous meeting. Captain Jack was indeed searching for any means to help his stricken passengers. "What do you think Captain Jack? Any ideas?" Garrett asked, after he had stealthily made his way over to the captain.

"Actually, yes, Garrett, I think I do have an idea. With the wind changing direction, I think if we have some of your Guardsmen, and any others who are able, hold up their life preservers or anything that would make a miniature sail, we might make land sooner."

At first, Garrett thought that Captain Jack had lost his mind, but since he had no idea of his own, he thought, "What do we have to lose?"

Aloud, he responded, "Okay, Captain Jack, I'll spread the word."

Both of them made it slowly around the creaking, crumbling hurricane deck, informing all of those who were able to raise their life preservers up and use them as sails. The life preservers were actually planks, about 5 feet long and a foot and a half wide and had ropes that could be used as handles.

Many on the improvised raft were able to do as directed, and shockingly to Garrett, Captain Wilson began to "sail" the raft. He could feel the increase in speed and he called out to Captain Jack, "It's working."

Captain Jack nodded in agreement, but he was also trying to assess the situation as a whole. During flashes of lightning, he was able to make out other bits of debris and smaller rafts dotted with people. The sails increased the speed of their raft so rapidly that soon they were leaving the others behind. As he continued to supervise the passengers, he growled to himself, "If we can get to shore before them, maybe we can find help for the others." Another thought crossed his mind. "I wonder where Davis and the rest of crew are."

Chapter 12

September 8, 1860

5:00 A.M.

Just about the time Captain Wilson was wondering about his crew, the first of the two boats that had been launched was about to make shore. Aboard were 13 people, the majority of them crew members who had boarded the boat originally to attempt to stop the leak. It was just getting light when they were able to see the shoreline. The overwhelming relief to see land was replaced in an instant with a disturbing site.

Huge breakers were smashing into the shoreline, and as luck would have it, the rowboat was headed to the one place along the shoreline between Chicago and Milwaukee where the bluffs were the highest and steepest, and there was almost no beach. Doubt entered the minds of the men. Had they endured the sinking, the storm, and huge waves, only to be smashed to bits against the rocks? As far as they could see, the breakers rolled fast and hard into the shore.

With the current controlling the boat, the crew had no choice but to hang on tight and hope for a miracle.

Hitting the very first breaker, the little boat flipped, tossing the men into the roiling water.

Thomas Shea, a Milwaukeean, was one of the first to struggle to shore. A giant wave tossed him toward the shore, and as he was pulling himself up, the undertow pulled him back out. A second wave tossed him ashore again, and he was able to grasp an exposed tree root and hold on. The porter of the *Lady Elgin*, Edward Westlake, washed up near him, and Thomas latched on to his neck and pulled him part way up the bluff.

Tim O'Brien, who had left his family to assist the crew, had been forced onto the rowboat as it was lowered, leaving his family to fend for themselves. Now, as he was struggling to remain afloat in the water and just about ready to give up, a wave pushed him close to shore, and Thomas Shea was again able to grasp on and pull him out of the massive surf. The porter lowered a tree branch, and Tim held on for dear life as he tried to regain some strength.

One by one the men struggled to shore and were able to scale the cliffs. The first few found a home nearby. They returned to the cliffs and pulled the others up with a rope that they had seized. Once all the men had made it, they found out where they had landed from the owners of the home, the Gages. They were just north of the town of Winnetka, Illinois.

The steward of the *Lady Elgin*, Fred Rice, wasted no time in finding out from the Gage family where the nearest telegraph office was. He set off as soon as he was able to get help. The others returned to the bluff, and in the gray dawn of the morning, the ship's clerk, H. G. Caryl, was able to spot numerous pieces of debris floating beyond the breakers, some with people holding onto them. About an hour after they had made it to shore, Edward Westlake pointed to the surf close to shore. There, the second boat was just reaching the breakers, and like the first, it tipped immediately, throwing the eight passengers into the maelstrom.

The first mate, George Davis, was aboard the second boat, and along with a young deck sweeper named Eddy Hogan were the first to make it safely to shore. The second mate, William Beeman, was not making progress nearly as well. He swam under the capsized boat to get a breath of air, and when he finally felt land under his feet, he yelled to the other two, "I can't stand up. Throw me a line!"

George went up the bluff in search of a rope, but by the time he returned, William had been able to struggle to shore on his own. Unfortunately, four of the others in the rowboat were not able to defy the odds, and they all drowned less than a hundred yards from shore.

The alarm had been raised, however. Once a message was telegraphed, people from Winnetka, Grosse Point, and even Northwestern University in Evanston, poured to the shore in hopes of helping rescue others. The sight they beheld left them nearly speechless and in shock. As far as the eye could see, well beyond the breakers, bits and pieces of the wreckage were scattered. More astonishing was the number of people clinging to those pieces of debris and praying to make it to the shore alive. Courage was about to be tested both by the passengers of the *Lady Elgin* and those on shore hoping to lend them aid.

*   *   *   *

Meanwhile, still well out in Lake Michigan and beyond the breakers, the survivors on the raft met with another disaster. A wave, much larger than the others that had already been pounding the raft, now came crashing down on top of the already bedraggled group. The raft, already weakened, split in two.

A scream was heard, and everyone turned to the spot on the raft where Ann Kennedy had been sitting. In an instant the mother of little 5 month old Mary Kennedy had disappeared. Johanna Rice, holding the little girl tightly in her arms, cried out in despair as the little girl's mother dropped from sight beneath the relentless power of the sea.

Once the inhabitants of the two rafts had somewhat recovered, they began to take inventory of who was still with them. On the smaller raft, Captain Jack eyed the group that remained. Garrett Barry, Willie, Willie P, the Jervises, John Crilley, and another woman named Margaret Hayes were the only people on the tiny little piece of wood decking.

"Garrett, this raft is too overloaded for this many people. I am going over to the larger raft where there is more room. I think it would be safer if someone else would be willing to come along as well." The last statement was for everyone on the raft.

"I'll come along," John Crilley replied.

Garrett shook his head and looked down at his son, who was now in great distress. Willie's breathing was erratic, and he was barely conscious. "I don't think he should be moved, Captain Jack. I will stay here with him." He turned to his son's friend. "William, why don't you go with the Captain to the other raft? There's very little you can do for him now."

"No, sir, I am not leaving my friend." There was a great determination in Willie P.'s voice. "I am staying right here, and I will get him to shore."

Garrett offered a grim smile to the boy and nodded, "Very well." He turned to Captain Jack and stated, "We three are staying here."

Margaret Hayes volunteered, "I will go across to the other raft, Captain Jack."

"Very well," the captain responded. "Okay, let's make our way as quickly as we can."

Captain Jack, John Crilley, and Margaret Hayes then slowly eased themselves off the raft and into the unforgiving water. The waves had lessened slightly, and the other raft was only a few yards away, so they were able to swim quickly to the other raft, where Michael Smith, a crew member, along with Thomas Keogh and a few of the Union Guardsmen pulled them aboard.

Once aboard, Captain Jack looked over the sea of water. He noted that were now only five on the small raft from where he had come. This larger raft held between 30 and 40 people, including the little baby that Johanna Rice still enfolded in her arms. Miraculously, the baby seemed none to worse for wear.

Captain Jack went over to Johanna. "How is she doing?"

Johanna replied, "Not badly, Captain. I think she will be alright if we can get to shore soon."

"Soon, very soon. Please hold on, Mrs. Rice. We can do this."

Johanna nodded at the Captain and then returned her attention to the little girl. Then an unexpected scream of anguish filled the morning air. All of the people on board the large raft turned their eyes to the smaller raft. What they were witnessing seared itself into their hearts and minds.

It was Willie P. who had let out the wail. He was holding Willie Barry in his arms and screaming, "No! Wake up, Willie! We're almost there. I can see land! Please wake up!"

Captain Jack looked across the expanse to Garrett Barry. Garrett just shook his head and with a downcast heart, attempted to console his son's friend. Willie Barry had died. Right there. Right in front of his father and his best friend. John and Margaret Jervis, the other two on board the undersized raft, also tried to help with the distraught boy.

They extricated Willie P. from the young boy he had been holding. "Willie P.," Margaret said to him, "you did everything that could be expected. Willie's wounds were just too serious."

As upset as he was, Willie P. was still determined to keep his promise. "Captain Barry," he sobbed, "I'm sorry about Willie, but we made a promise that we would make it to shore together. Would it be okay if I held onto him until we get there?"

Garrett, visibly shaken by this tragic loss, was still able to give some solace to Willie P. "Sure, Willie, just give me a moment with him, okay? Then you two can come to shore together, just like you promised." Garrett turned away from the other three at that point and bowed his head over his only son. Whether he was praying or just grieving, none of the three on the little raft knew. It was heart-wrenching to know they had come this far, only to lose the lad now.

Willie P., who by this time was being held by Margaret Jervis, continued to weep, but for a moment he was able to stop. He turned to Mr. and Mrs. Jervis, "Do you think Mary Anne and her parents are okay?"

"It's possible, Willie P.," John said to him consolingly. "They were on a small piece of the deck the last we saw, so it is very likely that they are still floating along, heading for shore, just like us." Over the top of Willie P.'s head, the couple glanced at each other's faces with raised eyebrows, and John gave his wife a helpless shrug of his shoulders and held out his hands, as if to say, "It's up to God now." Then they went back to tending Willie P.

*   *   *   *

Mary Anne Fahey and her parents were doing exactly what John Jervis had conveyed to Willie P. They were still floating along, and they were heading for shore, although with the change of wind direction, it seemed they were paralleling the shoreline, now visible in the morning light.

"Daddy, do you believe in curses?" Mary Anne asked Patrick, as they continued to grip their raft tightly in the ever pounding waves.

"Curses? No, not really. Why would you ask that, Mary Anne?"

Her mother Mary spoke up as well. "You mentioned that once before. What has you so engrossed in curses all of the sudden?"

Mary Anne paused for a moment, and then relayed the story that George Davis had told Willie and her. "So you can see why I might be thinking that," she finished quietly.

Patrick and Mary glanced at each other, and then Patrick responded, "Well, I don't know much about curses, Mary Anne, but I would say that our Irish luck seems to have gone missing of late. I guess our leprechaun forgot to board back in Chicago."

Despite the seriousness of the situation, the family managed smiles at each other. Hope once again filled Mary Anne's soul. If they could still smile after all that had beset them, then there still must be a chance to make it through this suffering alive.

"Okay," Patrick continued, "it has gotten light. At least we can see what we are doing. Let's keep a sharp eye out for anything or anybody that might help us."

Mary squinted at her husband and added, "It wouldn't hurt to say a prayer either."

"That, too," he agreed.

"That, too," Mary Anne echoed.

Chapter 13

September 8, 1860

9:00 A.M.

"Now boys, look out for the breakers ahead!" shouted Captain Jack. The raft upon which he and others floated was just about to reach shore, and the huge breakers that were still ferociously rolling into shore appeared to be the last hurdle for the exhausted passengers to endure.

Captain Jack was doing everything in his power to keep the spirits of those around him as positive as possible. He knew, as many did, that sometimes survival depended on the mental state, not the physical. Earlier, with many others on smaller rafts and pieces of debris within earshot of the large raft, he had encouraged everyone to shout, "Three cheers for light and land."

As Captain Jack scanned the area for others, he noted that Garrett Barry's small raft was still nearby. John Jervis, his wife Margaret, Willie P., and the body of Willie Barry were still all aboard. Willie P. had made good his promise to bring his friend to shore, and now they were only a couple of hundred yards from the goal.

"Listen, Willie P." Garrett told him. "You have been a loyal friend to Willie, and you have done all that anyone could require of you. When this raft overturns, do not hold onto him. Do you hear me? Promise me you will swim with all your being to make it to shore. Willie would understand. His body will wash ashore. Do you understand?"

Willie P. looked down at his friend, and then up at Garrett. "Yes, sir, I understand."

Garrett gave him a quick hug, and then turned to John and Margaret. "Are you two ready?" They nodded at Captain Barry, and as one, all four grasped on to the raft for support, looked toward shore, and waited.

Ahead of them, they could see the large raft entering the breakers. It was a terrible sight to witness, and fear swelled within them as they knew they were about to be next.

On board the large raft, Captain Jack turned to two women, Miss Frank Rivers and Minnie Newcomb. "Hold tight, ladies, you have come too far to be drowned."

The raft reached the first large breaker, and almost immediately some of its passengers, despite death grips on the raft, were tossed into the massive surf. One of them was Captain Wilson. Another was Johanna Rice, who had just taken back the baby, Mary Kennedy, from Margaret Burke, who had been holding her while Johanna adjusted herself for the rough ride.

Margaret, and her husband Edward, were still aboard the rapidly disintegrating raft after that first wave, so they were able to see Captain Jack gallantly straining to reach Johanna and the little baby. Just as he neared them, a large piece of debris from the broken raft struck him in the head. He sank beneath the waves and did not resurface. Margaret gasped and pointed, and her husband followed the direction of her hand.

Johanna Rice was still struggling to stay afloat, but another wave crashed down on her, and with the massive undertow pulling her under, both she and the baby submerged and were lost from sight.

"Dear God, help us!" Margaret cried out, as the piece of the raft carrying her and her husband was crushed by a following breaker that threw them into the churning vortex.

It wasn't God who would help them, although if there was ever a guardian angel sent by God, this one showed up in the person of one Edward Spencer. Having run all the way through fields and brush from Northwestern University, Edward Spencer had already pulled one person ashore, and being an excellent swimmer, he had made it down to the beach and was searching for anyone who might be nearing shore.

Spencer had seen all the people and debris floating just beyond the breakers just as he reached the bluffs, and he was able to scramble down to the shore just as Margaret and Edward were thrown from the raft, along with John Crilley, Thomas Keogh, and Martin Delaney.

Delaney cried out, "Get hold of me, for God's sake, or I will be drowned!" Despite his best efforts, John Crilley could not reach him, and Delaney disappeared beneath the waves. Crilley struggled to stay above water as the relentless undertow again and again sucked him under. He was able to grasp onto a plank, which brought him near shore. Struggling, he was able to see rescuers on shore throwing a rope toward him. Every time he tried to clamp on to it, his broken and battered hands failed him.

Someone yelled, "Grab it with your teeth!" Crilley managed to work the rope into his mouth, clamped down, and those on shore literally dragged him to shore with the rope securely in his mouth.

Edward and Margaret Burke, meanwhile, were thrashing in the surf. Edward watched his wife disappear from sight once, and in despair was ready to give up himself, when he saw her pop to the surface. Helping hands from Edward Spencer and others grasped their exhausted bodies and pulled them onto the sand. Margaret was so physically bruised, beaten, and exhausted that she could not move. Rescuers along the beach carried her to a farmhouse, and others assisted Edward Burke to his wife's side.

The two women, Frank Rivers and Minnie Newcomb, whom the captain had encouraged to hold tight just before he had been flung into the water, also struggled to endure the death trap of breakers and undertow. As they held onto a piece of the debris, and each other, Minnie called to her friend, "I'm going to drown."

"Hold on!" Miss Rivers shouted. "Hold onto me!"

Minnie gave her one last look and shook her head. "I won't take you with me." In an instant, another wave rushed her away from her friend and under the water.

Miss Rivers cried out, grief overtaking her, but with Herculean effort she somehow managed to reach the beach. Once there, and away from the pull of the water, anguish overcame her. The sights and sounds of so many dying kept replaying in her mind, and it was almost unbearable. She lay on the beach, gasping for breath, sobbing uncontrollably even as rescuers attempted to give her support.

Chapter 14

September 8, 1860

10:00 A.M.

Now it was the small raft with Garrett Barry and the others that entered the turbulence. John Jervis and his wife Margaret were tossed to one side of the raft, while Garrett and Willie P. were swept to the other side. Willie P. finally released his grip on the body of his friend when he realized he was unable to stay afloat with only one arm.

Garrett screamed, "Willie P., hang on!" He attempted to make his way to the youngster, and just as he reached for him a huge breaker carrying beams from the *Lady Elgin* crashed into both of them. In an instant both disappeared from view. Neither resurfaced.

John Jervis was holding his own in the thrashing water. He grasped onto Margaret, trying to pull her to the shore. The relentless undertow pulled her away from him. He felt his feet hit the bottom, and knowing he was close to shore, he dove after his wife. Again he was able to locate Margaret, and clutch one of her arms. It was a tug-of-war fight to the death between John and the water, and just as it appeared John would be the victor, another piece of debris struck him the shoulder. Pain shot through his body, causing him to release the vise like grip he had on his wife.

Margaret was immediately pulled back under, while John was actually pushed toward shore. Regaining his footing, he glanced at his arm to see if there was any major injury. Seeing none, he rushed back toward the waves, only to find that Margaret was nowhere in sight. John fell to his knees in both physical and emotional agony. Those on the beach came to his aid and gently led him away from the water and tended to his wounds.

Meanwhile, Edward Spencer continued to pull individual survivors from the water. Each time, he would stop by a fire that had been built by some of the rescuers in order to warm both survivors and rescuers. Each time his friends would tell him, "Edward, you've done enough. If you keep going back in there, you will die."

Another friend grabbed him, "Edward, you have gone in there 15 times. You can barely stand. Your head is bleeding. You must have been hit by something out in the water. Please stay here."

Edward was about to give in and collapse next to the fire when he glanced once more out toward the water.

What he spotted was a large piece of wood with a man's head protruding above it. A moment later he saw a woman's head pop up next to the man's. Adrenaline coursed through his veins, and he headed once again into Lake Michigan.

"Boys, it's a man trying to save his wife. I'm going to help him."

The two people that Spencer was going after were John and Ellen Eviston. John's brother Martin had made it to shore earlier by clinging to an overturned boat until he had reached the breakers, and then he had somehow managed to survive the waves and undertow until he reached the beach and collapsed. As Edward Spencer returned to the water to help John and Ellen, Martin was passed out in a rescuer's home.

John and Ellen had managed to survive in a most unlikely manner. After they had been tossed into the water from the storm, they had come across one of the paddle wheel covers. This huge wooden object turned out to be a lifeboat of a sort. Even though it was partially filled with water, the Evistons were able to pull themselves inside and be somewhat protected from the waves and storm.

However, once they reached the line of waves that were pounding the shore, they began to be tossed about inside the cover. The waves brought the cover very near the shore a number of times, but the current kept pulling it away. On one particularly large surge of water, Ellen was thrown violently into the side of the shell-like structure. Her head smashed against the wood, knocking her unconscious.

John realized it was now or never. He grasped his wife in one arm, waited for the next breaker to carry them close to shore, and then leapt out of the enclosure and into the water. On shore, Edward Spencer had been watching intently, trying to determine when it would be the most advantageous to enter the ever spiraling rollers. Just as Eviston jumped, Spencer saw the opportunity.

It was perfect timing. John saw Edward coming toward him. He adeptly switched his wife from the arm closest to shore to the one that faced the sea in order to grasp the saving hand of Edward Spencer. Edward, his strength nearly gone, towed the two survivors to shore, amid cheers from hundreds of lookers-on. Edward collapsed, unable to do anymore.

John Eviston saw that his wife was in dire straits, and he half-pulled, half-carried her to the nearest cabin, where fortunately a doctor from Chicago had just arrived to help in any way he could. Ellen was unconscious, and not breathing. The doctor did what he could, but could not find a pulse. He was about to declare her dead, and in frustration, or as a last ditch effort, he struck Ellen's feet with a pine board.

The shock from the blow somehow rejuvenated Ellen's pulse, and slowly she regained consciousness. Once he was sure that Ellen was going to be okay, John made his way back toward the shore to see if he could locate any other friends or relatives. In short order, he was reunited with his brother Martin.

That joyous reunion was short-lived, however, when Martin relayed the message that their relatives, Thomas Eviston and his wife Bridget, had not been so fortunate. It was a bittersweet moment, one that would be played out again and again as others from the *Lady Elgin* had to come to grips with the fact that they had survived while other loved ones had not.

Chapter 15

September 8, 1860

3:00 P.M.

On shore, searchers continued to comb the beach and scan the water for any more survivors. A number of bodies had already drifted ashore, and those who had survived had been taken in by locals and given food, clothing, and warmth. Some returned to the beach to assist and pray that more survivors could still be found. Others, like George Davis and H. S. Caryl, had made their way to the station in Evanston, and boarded a train for the quick journey to Chicago to find even more assistance for those involved in the disaster.

Survivors from the Milwaukee area made their way by train back to their home city. There they were met by a hoard of despondent relatives, looking for any information about their loved ones. Some congratulated the survivors, but almost immediately began firing questions at them. The stories from the survivors often brought howls of despair when loved ones realized that a family member had been lost.

A few of the survivors, after telling their tales, hurried home, changed clothes, and grabbed the next train back toward Winnetka and Evanston. One, Tim O'Brien, who had been on one of the two lifeboats that had been the first to make shore, was returning to the scene in search of his wife. As he reached the station, Michael Fahey, who had returned to Milwaukee after receiving news of the disaster, recognized him as one of the city's common councilmen.

"Tim, hold up," he called. "You didn't happen to see what became of my brother Patrick or his family, did you?"

"Sorry, Michael, I didn't. I was trying to help on the first life boat, and we were swept away from the ship. I have no idea about anyone, even my wife. That is why I am heading back."

"Understood," Michael nodded. "I am so sorry, Tim. I wish you and yours well."

"Thanks, Michael. Are you coming down on the train as well?"

Michael sighed, "Yes, I have Patrick's two boys out at the farm. We have been keeping it from them thus far. I want to make sure before we tell them anything."

"I understand completely. Well, then, let's go."

A special train had been voluntarily offered to allow Milwaukee citizens, including other members of the German Yagers, Guard members, and families of those on the *Lady Elgin*, to hurry to the site.

On the way, Tim filled Michael in on what he had seen and heard. "I was in the hall and told my wife and sister-in-law to stay, and I would go check out what had happened. Then I would come back for them. I was helping with the yawl, helping them lower it into the water. They were hoping that they could try to plug the hole with mattresses and whatever else we could find."

"So what happened?" Michael asked.

"Well, we lowered the boat, and the crew said to jump in, but I told them I needed to go back and get the rest of my group. They said that there wasn't time, and shoved me in the boat. The only problem was that the yawl only had one oar, so we couldn't make any headway with all the waves crashing down on us. Finally the crew gave up, and tried to head to shore to get help. All of us saw the *Lady Elgin* go down when we were just a few hundred yards off. We reached the bluffs near Winnetka about 4 or 5 in the morning, I'm guessing, and somehow all 13 of us in that little boat managed to survive the breakers and undertow once we were flipped off."

Michael shook his head sadly. "What a waste. I can only imagine what we will see, what they all went through."

Tim sadly shook his head, "No, Michael, you can't. There are no words to accurately describe it. No one in the Third Ward will go untouched by this. No one."

Michael, coming to a full realization of what Tim's words meant, stood dumbfounded. Tim's words echoed in his ears. "No one will go untouched."

Chapter 16

September 8, 1860

5:00 P.M.

"Dadddy, I am so tired. Is anybody going to help us?" Mary Anne's mind and body, exhausted by over 12 hours in the water, was at the point of capitulation.

Patrick, who had almost resigned himself and his family to a watery grave, heard his little daughter's plea, and once again adrenaline rushed through him, the overwhelming need to survive re-surfacing. As he continued to tightly grip the raft with one hand, he pulled his daughter onto his lap and pulled her close.

"I know, sweetie, I know. I would think by now somebody would realize what had happened and would come looking for us."

"I'm so hungry," Mary Anne murmured.

Her mother and father looked on helplessly as their daughter continued to weaken. Just when they were sure their luck had run out, Mary noticed some objects floating in the water nearby.

"Patrick, are those apples?" she queried. "It couldn't be," she continued in disbelief.

Patrick peered in the direction that Mary was pointing. Indeed, it did appear that there were pieces of fruit floating just out of reach. Patrick made a quick decision. Studying the waves, he decided that, while still strong, they had subsided enough where he felt he could brave them for a short distance and try to gather some of the floating bounty.

"Mary, hold on to Mary Anne," he ordered. "I am going after some of them."

He quickly transferred Mary Anne to her mother's lap, and then slipped into the water slowly, in order to not upset the small raft that was their lifeline. Patrick was a strong swimmer, and in a few moments he had reached the nearest object. It was an apple, just as Mary had thought. He quickly slid it inside his shirt and continued on to another. And another. And another. In short order, he had found six of the juicy orbs, and began to make his way back toward the small craft where the two females watched him anxiously.

Once he reached the raft, Patrick transferred the produce to his wife and daughter. He was about to pull himself up when he noticed another floating object not too far away. "No way," he muttered. He looked up at his wife and said, "I'll be right back. There's something else out there I want to investigate."

"Be careful, Patrick," she called. Mary's was concerned that the strain of swimming, added to all they had endured, would cause him to succumb. The thought of her husband and children's father dying right in front of her would be more weight than she could shoulder.

Patrick made his way over to the floating piece. It appeared to be made of wicker, and he thought at first it might be a small basket, but as he neared it, and was able to finally grasp it, he realized there floated a bottle with wicker encasing it. "Oh, could it really be…?" He quickly turned back to the raft and soon clambered aboard, holding his prize.

Despite the treacherous situation, Mary smiled when she recognized what the small object was. Mary Anne, however, was unsure what the bottle contained. As she devoured one of the apples, she asked, "What is it, Daddy?"

He grinned at his wife, "Medicine."

His wife just shook her head and produced a small laugh. "Medicine, my eye," she told her daughter. "It's whiskey, I imagine."

Mary had imagined correctly. It was a bottle of Irish whiskey which, along with the apples, had arrived fortuitously for the spent trio. Debris from the wreck of the *Lady Elgin* had followed them toward shore, and it had included both of those treasures. Patrick pulled out the cork, tilted the bottle to his lips, and allowed the strong aroma to reach his nostrils momentarily. The he poured some of the strong liquor into his mouth, swallowed, and shivered as the burn of the alcohol slowly made its way down his throat and began to send tendrils of warmth throughout his body.

It was a small relief to the agony, and Patrick took one more swig from the brown bottle and handed it to Mary. "Do it, it will help a little." She nodded, downed a mouthful of the brown liquid, and shivered too.

"Whew!" she stammered. "That's strong!" Patrick nodded. Mary took another swallow and handed the bottle back to Patrick. He held it for a moment, and then looked thoughtfully at his daughter, who was still munching on her first apple. Mary noted that glance and protested, "Patrick, no."

"I know, Mary. You know I would never normally do this, but this is an extreme situation. It will help ease some of the pain."

Mary Anne did not understand exactly what her parents were discussing, as she huddled against her mother for warmth and continued to gnaw away on her apple. She was quite surprised when her father extended the bottle toward her.

"Mary Anne, I want you to try something for me."

"What's that, Daddy?"

"I want you to take a small swallow of this. It will help you feel a little warmer." Mary Anne slowly reached for the bottle, and Patrick stopped short of handing it to her and added, "You might not like the taste of it, sweetie, so as soon as you swallow, take another bite out of your apple. Okay?"

"Okay, Daddy."

Mary Anne grasped the bottle from her father and slowly brought it to her lips. She had never been allowed to taste alcohol in her young life, but she had seen the adults drinking it often. The effect it had on some of them, especially when they had too much of it, both amused and frightened Mary Anne. She remembered laughing when some of her relatives had imbibed a bit too much, and struggled to walk in a straight line. On the other hand, she lived in the Third Ward, so she also knew the violence that sometimes occurred when people drank to excess.

Still, she trusted her father implicitly, so Mary Anne poured a small amount of the whiskey into her mouth, felt the burn on her tongue and mouth, smelled and tasted the oaken flavor, and then swallowed. She gagged almost immediately from the burning sensation that coursed deep down inside her. "Apple," her father reminded her quickly.

The shock of the liquor entering her system had made her momentarily forget the second direction her father had given her. She took a quick bite of the apple, and the delicious fruit somewhat covered the flavor of the whiskey in her mouth, but the powerful spirit continued to spread within her. She shivered involuntarily, but she did feel the warmth that her father had promised.

After the initial shock, Mary Anne was able to slowly relax and, had it not been for the continuous action of the waves, could have fallen asleep almost immediately. "Here," Patrick said to Mary, reaching for her daughter, "I'll hold onto her for a while." He pulled his only daughter into his arms as Mary pulled the bottle out of her hand.

"That's enough for her," she commented. However, Mary gave her husband a wry smile and downed another mouthful before handing the bottle back to him. He grasped the bottle, slammed a quick swallow, and then tossed the bottle back into the water.

"Maybe our luck is changing," he commented. "Food, whiskey, we're still alive, and we can see land. Maybe our little leprechaun finally decided to wake up and give us a hand."

"Daddy, are we going to make it to shore?"

"I hope so, honey. We just need the wind to push us in that direction." He frowned at his wife over the top of his daughter's head. Both the direction they were drifting, along with the sight of the breakers smashing into the shore, had both of them realizing that their struggle was far from over. "For now, eat another apple. You need your strength. We all do."

*   *   *   *

Tim O'Brien and Michael Fahey had made it back to the Winnetka area, and after asking a few questions they were able ascertain where bodies were being brought for identification. The corpses had been brought to the marshal's office in the court house.

Over 20 bodies were already there when the two men walked in. They steeled themselves for the unpleasant task ahead. As they walked from one to another, both had mixed emotions. They were hoping beyond hope that none of those were related to them, yet that would leave them wondering where their loved ones were. Still alive, floating on Lake Michigan? Or just… floating?

Suddenly, Michael heard Tim gasp and drop to one knee next to the body of a woman, who was lying there with a peaceful expression on her face, as if she was only sleeping. Michael did not know Tim's wife personally, but there was no doubt who this woman was. Michael placed his hand on Tim's shoulder. "I'm so sorry, Tim," he tried to comfort sadly.

~ 130 ~

Tim nodded, but there was no reply as he remained knelt next to his deceased wife. "I will give you some space," Michael stated. "I am going to keep searching."

"Thanks, Michael," a now despondent Tim managed to reply. "Good luck finding your family."

Michael left the grieving widower and continued to examine those remaining corpses that filled the room. He breathed a sigh of relief when he finished. He did not recognize any of them as Patrick, Mary, or Mary Anne. He decided to see if any other survivors were around and able to provide any more clues to the whereabouts of the missing Faheys.

He had no luck at first, but then he spoke to a survivor who had mentioned that someone had just been found alive near Evanston. Reinvigorated, he made his way to Evanston, just a couple of miles away, and after searching the area and asking anyone who might have some information, he was directed to the home of Paul Pratt, an Evanston resident, who had helped revive a man named Colonel H.W. Gunnison.

Colonel Gunnison had recovered enough to speak to Michael. He was dressing as Michael entered the room.

Gunnison informed him that he had drifted quite a ways south, and while he had not seen anyone else, he had noted that a good deal of wreckage had floated along with him this far south. Gunnison felt that it might still be possible for people to be out in the water, although with the gathering dusk, if they were not found before nightfall, the odds of survival through another night on the lake were minimal at best.

Those words spurred Michael to make his way quickly to the bluffs overlooking Lake Michigan. There he found a number of people watching the lake for any sign of life. They relayed a message to Michael that the tug *McQueen* had been dispatched to look for survivors and bodies, the latter of which they had found some, the former of which they had found none.

Michael was despondent. He was about to turn away from the great expanse of water when a shout went up. "Look! Way out there! Is that a raft with people on it?"

Michael peered into the distance, hoping beyond hope that whoever had shouted was indeed correct. In the gathering gloom of the night descending once again onto the Illinois shore, it did appear that there was something out there. Could it be survivors?

Michael, along with others, began to follow the drifting piece of the wreckage, shouting and waving in the direction of the raft. With the distance and the sound of the waves crashing, the voices must have been drowned out. There was no response or movement from the raft that suggested that anyone out on the lake could hear or see them.

"Please, God, push them toward shore before it's too late," he prayed. His prayers would go unanswered. Despite following the raft from along the bluffs for the next hour, the raft remained out of earshot. Much to Michael's despair, the raft was lost from sight as darkness settled on September 8, 1860.

Chapter 17

September 8, 1860

6:30 P.M.

The sun was sinking beyond the bluffs in the distance. Patrick, Mary, and Mary Anne Fahey huddled in the gathering darkness as they continued to float south on Lake Michigan. No aid was in sight.

The apples and whiskey had fortified the three for a short time, but now as the light faded, Mary began to weep quietly. "What about William and Charles Patrick?"

"They are in good hands, Mary," Patrick replied quietly. "Michael will take good care of them."

"Daddy, are we going die?" quavered Mary Anne, who was barely conscious, but still able to comprehend the conversation that her parents were having. A chill filled the Faheys, both from the autumn weather, and from the realization that their situation had gone from desperate to hopeless.

Patrick, doing what he could do to comfort his daughter, could only reply, "It's in God's hands now, little girl." He pulled his wife and daughter tightly to his chest and repeated, "It's in God's hands now."

Mary Anne burrowed her head into Patrick's chest. As blackness enveloped them, the little family was swept from sight.

Epilogue

So many questions followed the sinking of the *Lady Elgin*. Why did this tragedy occur? Who was to blame? How many perished? Did anything come from the investigation of the collision between the *Lady Elgin* and the schooner *Augusta of Oswego*? What happened to the survivors? And, of course, how much of this story is true and what became of the Faheys?

Here is what the research and investigation found. The *Lady Elgin* had left Chicago at about 11:30 on the night of September 7th, 1860. Captain Wilson was, indeed, concerned with the weather, but did acquiesce to the desires of the excursionists to return to Milwaukee that night.

Once aboard, many passengers continued the festivities in the lounge with dancing and drinking. About 2:00 a.m. the storm hit, which dampened the party a bit, but still they continued. The lanterns were dimmed, but were still aglow and visible. In the pilot house, one of the crew spotted a light in the distance.

That light turned out to be the schooner *Augusta*, on its way south to Chicago with a large load of lumber as its cargo. The sailing schooner was about a third the size of the

Lady Elgin, and its captain, Darius Nelson Malott, had sailed from Port Huron, Michigan, a week earlier. They were almost to their destination when the tragedy occurred. Sailing at almost 90 degrees to each other, and neither ship able to change directions at the last moment, a collision occurred.

The force of the schooner punctured a hole in the hull of the *Lady Elgin*, and the schooner's jib boom pierced the forward cabin, and then broke off as the waves pulled the *Augusta* back and away from the *Lady Elgin*.

The damage was done. The *Augusta* captain, thinking that his ship had taken the worst of the collision, called for the crew to head immediately to Chicago, in order to both assess the damage and report the collision. While sustaining some damage, they were not in danger of immediately sinking. Had they dropped anchor and waited to see how the *Lady Elgin* was managing, it is possible that many more lives could have been saved. Unfortunately, that is only speculation in light of what then occurred.

By the time the *Augusta* reached Chicago, the *Lady Elgin* had already sunk. It took only about 20 minutes for the waves to tear her apart, despite efforts by crew and passengers alike to stave off the water pouring into the boiler room and filling the hold. Captain Wilson, knowing the fate of his beloved ship, ordered crew and passengers to prepare for the sinking. Firemen from Milwaukee did attempt to chop loose the hurricane deck, and when the ship did finally sink beneath the waves, the hurricane deck popped back to the surface with possibly more than 100 people aboard. Others that were thrown into the water either quickly drowned or, if they were able to manage, reached the large deck or pieces of floating debris. One of the band members actually used his drum to keep himself afloat and rode it all the way to shore and to safety.

For the remainder of the dark, stormy night, many people were swept off and drowned, while others held on for dear life, and following the Captain's orders tried to remain as stationary as possible. Then it was survive until they reached shore or someone came to rescue them.

The sinking of the *Lady Elgin* on September 8, 1860, occurred because a perfect storm of prior events conspired against those on board the side wheel steamer. Had Governor Randall not confiscated the guns from the Union Guards, who were only upholding the Constitution by defending their country and refusing to secede from the Union, the excursion would not have been necessary, nor even planned. Many people were angry with Randall after the disaster, and had it not been for the election of Lincoln two months later, the secession of South Carolina and the other Southern states, and ultimately the Civil War, more retaliation may have occurred. Once the war started, talk of secession in Wisconsin abated, and the story of the *Lady Elgin* faded rather quickly into near anonymity, except along the western shore of the Great Lakes.

Today, many people have not even heard of the *Lady Elgin*, despite the tremendous loss of life. It is, by far, the greatest catastrophe on the Great Lakes, with approximately 300 perishing in the cold, dark waters. Only the *Eastland*, a passenger ship docked at the Clark Street Bridge in the Chicago River on July 24, 1915, in nearly the exact same place as the *Lady Elgin*, had a greater loss of life. Over 800 perished when the ship rolled over at the dock and trapped the passengers inside the ship.

The *Lady Elgin* broke into many pieces, and a large portion of the upper deck work floated to shore and was scavenged for years. The boilers and engine, along with other parts of the ship, sank quickly and were lost for over 130 years. Trying to find her was akin to finding the Holy Grail of shipwrecks on the Great Lakes. It would not be until 1994 that she was finally discovered by a man name Harry Zych. Then the case of ownership caused a long, drawn out court case. Today, divers may, with permission, explore what is left of the wreckage.

Ships such as the *Titanic, Lusitania, U.S.S. Arizona,* and even the *Edmund Fitzgerald* have been more widely publicized and researched. The fact that this event was directly related to Civil War history, and the mood of the nation at that point in time, only emphasizes the importance of remembering this calamity, as well as scrutinizing the people involved and the decisions they made that influenced the outcome of this episode.

Both Captain Jack Wilson, who was pressured into sailing on a night where he knew the weather was dicey, and Captain Garrett Barry of the Union Guard, who was insistent upon leaving Chicago, both had a hand in the sinking of the *Lady Elgin*. And what of Captain Malott, the skipper of the *Augusta*? The sailing schooner was overloaded with lumber, and in the storm, the ship still had sails up, leaving maneuverability almost impossible. As commander of the *Augusta*, he needs to bear some responsibility as well.

Neither of the crew members on either ship advised anyone that they had seen the lights of the other until it was too late. Witnesses bear out that each had seen the other more than 20 minutes before the collision, yet neither changed course. Four years after the event, a law was passed that required all sailing vessels to carry running lights. If the schooner already had the fifteen dollar lantern on board, perhaps the crew members would have made better, or at least quicker, decisions to re-route their ships.

Captain Malott and his crew were put on trial for navigational negligence and the second mate on the *Augusta* was found to be incompetent, but none ever faced prison time. Some supporters of those aboard the *Lady Elgin* did not feel justice had been served, and tried to take matters into their own hands in the form of vigilante justice. They were intent on hanging the crew for not only their part in the collision, which some thought was done purposefully, but also for not checking to see if the *Lady Elgin* was still seaworthy and abandoning the hundreds of passengers on board her.

Fortunately, cooler heads prevailed, but in a twist of fate, just a few years later, Malott and most of his crew, who had long since left the *Augusta*, were aboard another

Great Lakes vessel, the *Mojave*. It disappeared mysteriously while on Lake Michigan. Some say it sank in a storm, but others think that vengeance was served, and the crew was hanged.

The *Augusta* itself was under such public objection that the owners changed its name to the *Captain Cook* and painted it black, but that did not stop it from being recognized. It was considered a cursed ship, and it eventually sank years later after striking a shoal in Lake Erie.

For the survivors and family members of those who had died, it was a long, painful period of funerals and memorials. Captain Jack Wilson's body was found a week later, and a memorial service was held in Chicago, at the very Wigwam some of the excursionists would have visited the day before the collision. His remains would then be taken to Coldwater, Michigan, where his final burial service and interment occurred.

Captain Barry's body was found a full two months later, near Michigan City, Indiana, on November 8th, along with a number of others. The changing seasons and currents in Lake Michigan caused numerous bodies to float for weeks and end up on shores very distant from Winnetka and Evanston. Barry's body was delivered to Milwaukee, and perhaps one of the largest funerals and processions in the history of Milwaukee ensued, as he was finally interred at Calvary Cemetery in Milwaukee. Numerous other Irish-Catholic victims were buried nearby, and many headstones in the cemetery honor those who lost their lives aboard the *Lady Elgin*.

Willie Barry and Willie Pomeroy both died that day, although there is some debate if Willie Barry made it to the breakers alive. One newspaper article stated that, according to survivor John Jervis, Willie Pomeroy had held onto Willie's lifeless body until they reached the shoreline, but another article stated that Willie Barry and his father perished together, fighting the waves and the undertow that pulled so many back into the tumultuous water just as they had thought they were going to make it to land. Either way, both boys lost their lives, their bodies were recovered, and they were buried at Calvary Cemetery in Milwaukee as well.

Shortly after the tragedy, in early 1861, Garrett Barry's pregnant wife, Mary, gave birth to a girl. The infant was named Garitha (also spelled Garetta in some records), in honor of the father she never knew. Mary would eventually move to St. Paul, Minnesota, where she would live until her death. However, according to records, she was returned to Milwaukee and buried next to her husband. Garitha would marry a man named George Nash, and then eventually they would have a son. They named him Garrett Barry Nash. She is also buried with her father at Calvary.

Edward Spencer, one of the heroes of the day, saved nearly 20 people. That heroism cost him dearly, as the physical and psychological damage he incurred changed him forever, creating almost an invalid from one who had been a healthy, active person. He was reported to have said to his brother William, after being totally exhausted from his efforts, "Will, did I do my duty? Did I do my best?" No one could disagree that he had, indeed, done all he could have possibly managed to save so many. A plaque at Northwestern University bears his name and tells of his heroic rescues.

The collision between the *Lady Elgin* and the *Augusta* resulted in the loss of around 300 individuals, with 96 passengers surviving. Of the 300 lost, at least 100 were within yards of the shore. The size of the waves, estimated from 12-20 feet high, combined with an intensely strong undertow, compounded by the exhaustion the waterlogged passengers felt after hours of struggle, made them fall victim to a merciless sea.

One survivor, George Lucas Hartsuff, became a Civil War general for the Union following the shipwreck. He had boarded in Chicago and was heading to Mackinac Island when he was caught in the chaotic incident. Five years earlier, he had cheated the Grim Reaper when, in a battle in Florida, he was shot. The bullet passed through his arm and lodged in his chest. To survive a battle wound and a shipwreck, and then to continue to serve his country in the bloodiest of all American wars, and survive through it as well, would be considered by some to be a stroke of good fortune. His luck would run out, eventually, as he passed away in 1874 from complications due to the bullet still being embedded in his body.

Another survivor, John H. Miller, would also serve honorably in the Union Army during the Civil War, as part of the 1st Wisconsin Artilley. He would later be buried at Forest Home Cemetery.

John Crahan had chosen not to go on the excursion, but his sister Mary had, and she would perish in the breakers. Margaret Hayes, one of only eight women to survive, lost her brother William that night. John and

Margaret found solace in each other, and after they had grieved over their lost loved ones, were actually married and lived a long and happy life together. Margaret would actually turn out to be the longest living survivor. The only married couples who both survived were the Burkes and the Evistons.

So who exactly are the Faheys? All of them were real people, and the history of how they came to Milwaukee and the jobs Patrick held are accurate. They did live on the corner of Detroit (now St. Paul) Avenue and Milwaukee Street, and the Barrys were their neighbors around the corner on Jefferson Avenue. Unfortunately, on September 8th, 1860, all three of them perished. Because there are no eyewitness accounts mentioning any of the three Faheys, what actually transpired in their last hours is purely conjecture.

They could have died when the *Lady Elgin* sank, as many others no doubt had. They could have clung to pieces of wreckage, only to be drowned by massive waves. It's entirely plausible, and very likely, they were aboard one of the rafts that had been the hurricane deck, only to be swept off by the rollers or even making it to shore, only to lose the battle at the very end. The story of watchers on shore seeing three people on a raft as darkness fell is true. No one knows who the three were, or what became of them, consequently the use of that particular event in this story.

So why use the Faheys at all? What makes them more noteworthy than any of the others who lost their lives? Nothing really, but to this author, they were family. Patrick Fahey's brother, Michael, was this author's great-great-great grandfather. Michael took it upon himself to adopt Patrick's and Mary's two boys, William and Charles Patrick, and raised them at the homestead in Richfield, Wisconsin.

During the inquest made by the coroner in Chicago, Mary Fahey was identified as Inquest #20, although in a newspaper article there was mention made that it could have also been a woman named Mary Mahoney. Since Mary Fahey's maiden name was Duffy, there could be no doubt that the list did not accidentally have Mary duplicated, as some others were. Further investigation showed that it was indeed her body that was found, as she was identified by her brother, C.M. Duffy, who lived in Chicago at that time. Her remains were sent to Milwaukee on September 13, 1860.

It is not known if Michael Fahey traveled to Chicago to search for his brother. Patrick was not fortunate enough to be recognized immediately upon being discovered. In fact, he was misidentified as Mr. Allan Williams, when his body was found a month and a half later, on October 27 near Whiting, Indiana. When the inquests ended on October 30, it appeared that Patrick's body had not been found, so he was officially listed as missing. However, on November 13th, after being exhumed a second time, he was positively identified, and thus returned to Milwaukee as well.

Now comes the mystery. After countless hours researching, emailing, and hunting through graveyards, neither of the graves of Patrick or Mary Fahey has been found. Records from 1860 tend to be sketchy and inconsistent at best, and no mention of their names show up in the records from the Archdiocese of Milwaukee, while many of the others from the *Lady Elgin* are listed. Cemetery records are also unclear and imprecise.

It seems a shame that there is no closure to this mystery. Many tombstones from that time have weathered away and have become almost unreadable, as the photos in this book bear out. Others may have just been wooden markers that have rotted away over time. There are locations in both St. Columbo Cemetery in Richfield and at Calvary Cemetery and Forest Home Cemetery in Milwaukee, where graves are known to be, but have no markers whatsoever. It is very possible that Patrick and Mary lay in one of those. This author will continue to search for any clues that may finally reveal the answers that are so ardently desired.

There is one more mystery that will probably never be solved. Ten-year old Mary Anne Fahey's body was never found. Perhaps she still lies beneath the waters of Lake Michigan. It is unlikely that anyone will ever know what became of the little lost lady.

Acknowledgements

Special thanks to:

Steve Schaffer, from the **Milwaukee Historical Society,** for assisting me with addresses of the Faheys and the Barrys, as well as geographical locations in the city of Milwaukee in 1860.

Carl Baehr, author and historian from Milwaukee, who researched and solidified the list of those who survived and those who perished, as well as personally sharing his research about the Faheys.

Valerie Van Heest, author of *Lost on the Lady Elgin*, as well as an underwater shipwreck explorer, whose research and writing provided many of the details needed to complete this book.

Barbara Meyer, Sheryl Meyer-Patzke, Susan Larson, and Luella Hunt, relatives who provided historical family documents from the Faheys, including maps from the 1860s, adoption papers for the Fahey boys, and a list of the Patrick Fahey family possessions that Michael Fahey retrieved from the 3rd Ward home.

Marge Holzbog, from the **Richfield Historical Society,** for assisting me with information about the Fahey family in Richfield, Wisconsin.

Cathedral of St. John the Evangelist, Milwaukee, Wisconsin, for providing documents about those parishioners lost on the *Lady Elgin*.

Tane Beecham, from the **Winnetka Historical Society**, for access to many of the documents from this tragedy.

Bob Giese and Margaret Berres, from **Forest Home Cemetery**, for their assistance with both the cemetery records and assistance in locating graves.

Photo Gallery

Memorial in the 3rd Ward, Milwaukee, Wisconsin, near the

dock where the *Lady Elgin* departed.

Author photo.

The only two known photos of the *Lady Elgin*.

Photo taken September 7, 1860, at the dock in Chicago.

Photo taken in Northport, Michigan.

Both photos courtesy of U-M Library Digital Collections. Great Lakes

Maritime Database.

Accessed: December 24, 2017.

The Survivors

Author photo.

Included here are the names of the known survivors from the *Lady Elgin*, along with any information found and/or photos taken by the author. Cemeteries are in italics

Aylward, William
Calvary
Block 5A, Lot 493

Boyd, Francis
Forest Home
Section 33, Lot 289

Burke, Edward & Margaret
Calvary
Block 7D, Lot 426

Crilley, John J.
Calvary
Block 9B, Lot 3
Union Guard Member

Dever, William
Calvary
Block 18 Lot 47

Doebert, Adelbert
Union
Block 1, North Side

 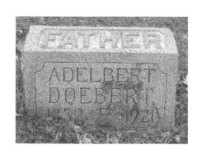

Eviston, John & Ellen
Calvary
Block 8, Lot 37

Eviston, Martin
Calvary
Block 7B, Lot 132

Furlong, George
Calvary
Block 6D, Lot 356

Hogan, Eddy
Calvary
Block 4E, Lot 24

Kinsella, William
Calvary
Block 6A, Lot 207

McLinden, John
Calvary
Block 6A, Lot 215

McManus, James
Calvary
Block 4A, Lot 152

Mellon, Ed
Calvary
Block 5B, Lot 212
Union Guard Member

Miller, John
Forest Home
Section D, B2, Lot 4
Civil War Veteran

Murray, John
Calvary
Block 6A, Lot 155

O'Brien, John
Forest Home
Section 44, B2, Lot 5

O'Brien, Tim
Calvary
Block 7C, Lot 269

Rodee, Jerome B.
Forest Home
Section 32, B17, Lot 2

Rogers, James
Forest Home
Section 4, B53, L15

Roper, John H.
Calvary
Block 16, Lot 123

Rossiter, John
Calvary
Block 17, Lot 6
Union Guard Member

Shea, Thomas
Calvary
Block 11C, Lot 42

Snyder, Fred
Forest Home
Section LP, B58, Lot 5

White, Edward
Forest Home
Section 35, Lot 158

The remaining survivors:

Ahearn, Ann
Aylward, Phillip
Beeman, William   Crew-2nd Mate
Bellman, James   from Eagle Harbor, MI
Beverung, Charles   German band member
       Rode his drum to shore
Bradford, W.   from Brunswick, OH
Caryl, H.S.   Crew-ship's clerk
Christianson, Frank H.
Collins, John H.   Crew-2nd pantry man
Connors, Michael   Lost in Lake Michigan 1871
Cook, James   from Stockbridge, WI
       Lost mother and sister

Crother, Terry   Crew-from Chicago, IL
Cummins, Thomas   Crew-from Chicago, IL
Darnes, William A.   Crew- from Chicago, IL
Davis, George   Crew-1st Mate, from Chicago, IL
Dempsey, Robert
Devarsky, Frederick
Doyle, John   buried at *Calvary*-Block 6A, Lot 55
       (no headstone)

Duffy, William
Gardner, H.G.
Gilmore, Denny
Grear, Robert   Crew-from Buffalo, NY
Gunnison, G.W.
Hartsuff, George L.   Fort Mackinac, MI
       Civil War Veteran
Hayes, Margaret   loses brother William,
       marries Mary Crahan's brother
Herbert, John   Union Guard Member
Hetherman, John   Crew-from Chicago, IL
Hoepner, Fredrick   from Two Rivers, WI
Jacobsen, John   from New York, NY
Jarvis, John   loses his wife, Margaret
Kennedy, Thomas
Keogh, Bridget

Keogh, Thomas
Kingsley, Issac   buried at *Forest Home*-Section 32
                           Block 3 Lot 6 (no headstone)
Kuetenmeyer, Fredrick
Leverenz, Leopoldine   buried at *Forest Home*-Section 23
                           Block 52, Lot 4 (no headstone)
Loutz, Mrs. John   Lost husband and three children
Maher, Patrick
May, Charles
McCredan, Terry   Crew
McDonough, T.E.   from Detroit, MI
McLaughlin, Charles B.
Mills, William   from Ohio
Moots, William   from Lansing, MI
Murphy, Thomas   Crew-watchman
                           Moved to Random Lake, WI
Myers, Patrick   from Chicago, IL
Nelson, Edward
O'Leary, Catherine
O'Neil, John
Owens, Patrick
Parks, George
Powers, E.J.
Pritchard, Thomas
Regan, John
Rice, Fred   Crew-Steward, from Chicago, IL
Rivers, Miss Frank
Rollins, Frank
Rooney, Unknown
Roughan, Martin   Union Guard Member
Simonds, William
Singer, William   from Joliet, IL
Smith, Michael C.   Crew-from Ontonagon, MI
Steinke, Louis
Sullivan, Hugh   buried at *Calvary*-Block 5C, Lot 118
                           (no headstone)
Updike, Lyman   from Waupun, WI
                           Civil War Veteran

Walsh, Peter   buried at *Calvary*-Section 6B, Lot 104
                      (no headstone)
Westlake, Edward   Crew-Porter, from Milwaukee, WI
Winslow, Edward   Crew-from Chicago, IL

Those Lost on the

Lady Elgin

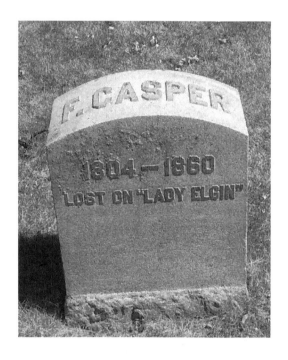

Author photo.

Many, but not all, of the victims of the sinking of the *Lady Elgin,* were found and identified. The following is the most up-to-date list the author has been able to construct, including photos of any headstones found in the greater Milwaukee area. Some victims, including Captain Jack Wilson, were returned to families in places such as Michigan, Kentucky, Louisiana, greater Wisconsin, and even London, England.

Calvary Cemetery-Milwaukee, WI

Barry, Captain Garrett
Block 6C, Lot 301
Age: 44
Union Guard Commander

Black, Hugh
Block 6B, Lot 168
Age: 29

Casper, Francis
Block 6A, Lot 78
Age: 56

Crahan (Crean), Mary
Block 7, Lot 381
Age: 19

Cumerford, Richard E.
Block 7B, Lot 34
Age: 18

Curtin, Elizabeth
Block 6A, Lot 214
Age: 21

Dwyer, Elizabeth
Block 6A, Lot 201
Age: 40

Engelhardt, John P.
Block 6A, Lot 121
Age: 45

Hackett, James
Block 6D, Lot 283
Age: 20

Handly, Matthew
Block 6A, Lot 204
Age: 17
Union Guard Member

Handly, Susan
Block 6A, Lot 204
Age: 20

Hendrickson, John
Block 6B, Lot 31
Age: 23

Horrigan, Michael
Block 7C, Lot 301
Age: 19

Jarvis, Margaret
Block 6B, Lot 168
Age: 21

Johnson, Charles
Block 6B, Lot 352
Age: 17

Keogh, Agnes
Block 6B, Lot 168
Age: 17

Lanigan, Michael
Block 6A, Lot 113
Age: 29

Matthews, Mary
Block 7C, Lot 341
Age: 27

McCormick, Francis
Block 6D, Lot 347
Age: 25

McCormick, Martha
Block 6D, Lot 347
Age: 19

McGill, Thomas
Block 7D, Lot 322
Age: 39

McGrath, Mary
Block 5E, Lot 72
Age: 22

McLaughlin, Elizabeth
Block 6A, Lot 83
Age: 20

Monaghan, Andrew
Block 6B, Lot 98
Age: 27

Monaghan, Catherine
Block 6B, Lot 98
Age: 22

Monaghan, Patrick
Block 6B, Lot 98
Age: 64

Murphy, Sarah
Block 7, Lot 348
Age: 17

Neville, Thomas
Block 5B, Lot 179
Age: 27
Union Guard Member

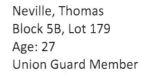

O'Leary, Daniel
Block 6A, Lot 186
Age: 40

Pollard, Alice
Block 6B, Lot 161
Age: 22

Pollard, John
Block B, Lot 161
Age: 30

Pomeroy, William C.
Block 7D, Lot 292
Age: 15

Purtell, Michael
Block 7B, Lot 43
Age: 26

Walsh, Patrick
Block 11B, Lot 82
Age: 20

The following are also listed as interred at Calvary. However, they have either no headstone or are unverified:

Ahearn, Margaret (28)	Block 1, Row 31, Lot 23
Barry, William (12)	Block 6C, Lot 301
	(likely with Garrett Barry)
Bohan, Catherine (22)	Block 1, Row 13, Lot 12
Cline, Patrick (26)	Block 1, Row 25, Lot 11
Cudahy, Steven (32)	Block 1, Row 11, Lot 13
	(Union Guard Member)
Duffy, James (40)	Block 1, Row 10, Lot 13
Eviston, Bridget (28)	Block 7B, Lot 132
Eviston, Thomas (31)	Block 7B, Lot 132
Flynn, Anna (13)	Block 1, Row 1, Lot 9
Gilligan, Ann (28)	Block 1 Row 12, Lot 12
Kennedy, Ann (20)	Block 6A, Lot 118
Kennedy, Mary J. (5 mos.)	Block 6A, Lot 118
O'Brien, Richard (15)	Block 1, Row 11, Lot 12
Schehan, Thomas (30)	Block 1, Row 2, Lot 9
Taflin, Mary (45)	Block 2, Lot 27 Row 4

Forest Home Cemetery-Milwaukee, WI

Oakley, George
Section 16, Block 27, L7
Age: 37

Parsons, Oliver Morris
Section 16, Block 27, L9
Age: 18

Phillips, William B.
Section 27, Block 18, L14
Age: 18

Plankinton, Eli
Section 31, Block 7, L3
Age: 15

Smith, William
Section 19, Block 6, L1
Age: 43

Struett, Herman
Section 23, Block 44, L3
Age: 47

Townsend, Milton
Section 14, Block 2, L5
Age: 20

Viig, Line
Section 16, Block 10, L1
Age: 24

Viig, Martha
Section 16, Block 10, L1
Age: 25

Warner, Edward
Section 16, Block 2, L4
Age: 26

The following are buried at *Forest Home Cemetery*, but do not have headstones:

Arnold, George (15)   Section 31, Block 3, Lot 9
Campion, John (27)   Section 16, Block 4, Lot 2
Chamberlain, Frank (59)   Section 16, Block 27, Lot 2
Corbett, Alexander (33)   Section 17, Block 1, Lot 4
Downer, Samuel (18)   Section B, Block 6, Lot 6
Leverenz, Otto (48)   Section 23, Block 52, Lot 1
Persons, Henry (16)   Section 14, Block 4, Lot 12
Potter, Edward (23)   Section 17, Block 3 Lot 2
Quail, John (28)   Section 17, Block 3, Lot 3

Other graves found in the greater Milwaukee area:

Cosgrave, James
Section 1, Block 105
Age: 16
St. James Cemetery
Kenosha, WI

Evarts, Charles
Row 4, Grave 99
Age: 27
W. Granville Cemetery
Granville, WI

Farnsworth, William
Section 1
Age: 64
Wildwood Cemetery
Sheboygan, WI

Grady, Michael
Row 16, Grave 5
Age: 44
St. Michael's Cemetery
Brown Deer, WI

Muller, Christian
Section NW B, Block 122
Age: N/A
Green Ridge Cemetery
Kenosha, WI

Nickel, Christian
Section 3, Lot 3
Age: 35
Union Cemetery
Milwaukee, WI

Smith, Franklin
SE Corner
Age: 19
Sunnyside Cemetery
Lannon, WI

The remaining victims and any additional information found. Coroner Inquest Numbers (IN) and records from the Archdiocese of Milwaukee (AM) are included:

Ahearn, Dennis (28)	IN #52, AM
Ahearn, Patrick (17)	
Alexander, Richard (NA)	IN #25, Crew-2nd Engineer From Chicago, IL
Barron, Ann (30)	
Bass, Henry (19)	
Bellew, James (46)	from Jackson, WI
Birmingham, Cornelius (19)	
Bishop, Augustus (16)	
Bishop, Henry (18)	
Bloos, Phillip (26)	IN #81
Bohan, Timothy (2)	
Bohan, Thomas (28)	
Bond, Eliza (28)	from Mineral Point, WI
Bond, Eliza Jane (9)	from Mineral Point, WI
Bond, Nathan (8)	from Mineral Point, WI
Bossenburg, Fred (25)	
Boulger, Ann (18)	AM
Boulger, Margaret (19)	AM
Bulfin, Thomas (35)	
Bungard, Thomas (24)	IN #112
Burke, Mary (24)	AM
Burns, Fanny (26)	
Burns, James (16)	IN #7.1, AM
Burns, Michael (30)	
Burns, William (27)	IN #108, Constable 4th Ward
Butler, Catherine (22)	AM
Canning, Patrick (29)	IN #104, AM
Casey, Dennis (14)	
Churchill, William (25)	
Codd, Bridget (23)	from Chicago, IL
Codd, Margaret (20)	IN #95, AM
Collins, James (21)	

~ 178 ~

Connaughty, Peter (17)
Connolly, James (34) IN #96, AM
Connolly, Patrick (36) IN #118
 Union Guard Member

Connolly, Terence (22) AM
Conway, John (13)
Cook, Eliza (24) IN #19.1
 from Stockbridge, WI

Cook, Jane (46) from Stockbridge, WI
Corcoran, Unknown
Coughlin, John (24)
Cuddehea, James (10)
Cullen, Eliza (20) from Watertown, WI
Delaney, Martin (33)
Delaney, Mary (27) AM
Delaney, Patrick (26) AM
Delury, Ellen (24) IN #79
Delury, John (24)
Diehl, Elias (NA) Crew-Carpenter
Dilersick, M. (42) IN #62
Donovan, Mary (19) IN #5, AM
Dooley, Martin (36) IN #102, harbormaster
 Union Guard Member

Dressler, William (19) IN #1, AM
Duffy, Margaret (19) IN #132
Dunner, Hannah (23)
Dwyer, Ellen (15) AM
Dwyer, Michael (44) AM
Eichorn, Gustav (21)
Ellis, Mary (32)
Fahey, Mary Anne (10)
Fahey, Mary (30) IN #20
Fahey, Patrick (35) Constable 3rd Ward
Fanning, Catherine (15) AM
Fanning, Elizabeth (20)
Faraby, George (35)
Faraby, Mary (24) AM

Fitzgerald, Ann (20)	IN #89, AM
Fitzgerald, Ann (20)	AM
Fitzgerald, Maurice (17)	
Fitzgerald, Patrick J. (19)	IN #119, AM
Fitzpatrick, Edward (23)	IN #35, Crew
	From Willow Springs, IL
Flanders, George (30)	
Foley, Bridget (22)	IN #91
Foley, Paul (45)	IN #121, AM
	Union Guard Member
Foley, William (20)	AM
	Union Guard Member
Gannon, Margaret (18)	
Garth, Amanda (26)	IN #3, from Paris, KY
Garth, Anna (23)	from Paris, KY
Garth, Mary (40)	from Paris, KY
Garth, William (45)	IN #107, from Paris, KY
Goetz, Daniel W. (42)	
Goff, Homer (16)	IN #16, from Racine WI
Grade, Ernest (8)	
Grade, Mary (26)	IN #142
Hall, B.F. (47)	
Hanna, Theodore (22)	
Hanson, Julia (14)	
Hanson, Louiza (21)	
Hayes, William (18)	IN #50
Hett, Fred (31)	
Hipelius, Godfrey (21)	
Hock, Christian (NA)	
Hopkins, Lydia (32)	from Eagle River, WI
Hopkins, Willie (3)	IN #54,
	from Eagle River, WI
Horan, John (30)	IN #74,
	Deputy Fire Marshal
Horner, William (20)	IN #92
Hoy, Ann O'Brien (30)	
Hubby, William (56)	from Rochester, NY

Humbert, Sarah (25)	from Chicago, IL
Humbert, Theodora (8)	from Chicago, IL
Ingram, Herbert (49)	IN #31.1
	from London, England
Ingram, Herbert Jr. (15)	from London, England
Jothum, Charles (23)	from Chicago, IL
Kelly, John (31)	IN #63
Kennedy, Phillip (18)	
Kilroy, Bridget (27)	
Kilroy, James (28)	Union Guard Member
Kilroy, May Cecilia (1)	AM
Kitto, Elizabeth (31)	from Mineral Point, WI
Kitto, Elizabeth (7)	from Mineral Point, WI
Kitto, Jane (12)	from Mineral Point, WI
Kitto, Mary (3)	from Mineral Point, WI
Kitto, Sophia (4)	from Mineral Point, WI
Komarick, Anton (20)	City Band Member
Komarick, Franz (23)	
Komarick, Joseph (17)	
Lacy, Charles (40)	IN #164
Lasky, Unknown (NA)	
Ledden, Amelia (21)	IN #40, AM
Locke, George R. (29)	IN #126
Loutz, John (NA)	from Chicago. IL
Loutz, Child (NA)	from Chicago, IL
Loutz, Child (NA)	from Chicago, IL
Loutz, Child (NA)	from Chicago, IL
Lumsden, Emma (4)	IN #70
	from New Orleans, LA
Lumsden, Francis A. (49)	from New Orleans, LA
Lumsden, Frank (16)	from New Orleans, LA
Lumsden, Mrs. Francis (32)	from New Orleans, LA
Lumsden, Servant (NA)	from New Orleans, LA
Lynch, Bloss (19)	
Malone, James (19)	IN #110, AM
	Union Guard Member
Maloney, Mary (19)	

McDonough, Patrick (40)
McGarry, Hugh (35) — AM, Union Guard Member

McGee, Ann (18) — IN #9
McGrath, Nicholas (32) — IN #12, Union Guard Member

McGrath, Patrick (17) — IN #32.1
McKay, William (15)
McLaughlin, Hanora (24) — IN #15, AM
McManus, Sarah (26) — IN #43
Meyer, Wilhelm (NA)
Morgan, Effort (21) — IN #67, Crew- from Erie, PA

Morrison, John (NA) — IN #2, from Racine, WI

Morton, Joseph (65) — IN #27
Murphy, James (28) — IN #99, AM, Union Guard Member

Murphy, Michael (35) — IN #53, AM
Murphy, Steven (28) — IN #32, AM
Newcomb, Minnie (NA) — IN #24
Newton, John M. (32) — IN #8 from Superior, WI
Nichols, Jacob (27) — Leader of City Band
O'Brien, James (22) — IN #82
O'Brien, Mary (24)
O'Brien, Michael (19) — AM
O'Grady, Anne (29)
O'Grady, John (30)
O'Grady, William (NA)
O'Leary, Jeremiah (5) — AM
O'Mahoney, Cornelius (35) — AM, Teacher, Union Guard Member

O'Neil, Thomas (22) — IN #111, AM, Union Guard Member

Patterson, Albert (17)
Pengally, Emma (12) — IN #11
Pentany, James (35)

Persons, John (17)
Phillip, August F. (63)
Pierce, Andrew M. (34)
Pine, Andrew (34)
Pine, Leveritia (20)
Quinlon, Patrick (24) — IN #87, AM
Rapp, Jacob (33) — IN #106
Reynolds, George F. (19) — IN #122, AM
Rice, Charles (7) — IN #39, AM
Rice, James (37) — AM, School commissioner 3rd Ward

Rice, Johanna (36) — IN #33, AM
Rich, Michael (NA) — IN #26, from Chicago, IL
Ries, Anton (49)
Riley, Peter (38) — IN #10, AM
Ring, Robert (32)
Ring, Sara Murphy (32)
Rogers, Edward (18) — IN #31, AM
Rooney, Christopher (25) — IN #65, AM
Rooney, John (30)
Rooney, Patrick (17)
Rooney, Sarah (26)
Ryan, Bridget (30) — AM
Ryan, James (30) — AM
Ryan, John (24) — AM
Ryan, Robert (26) — IN #99, AM

Salzner, Margaret (20) — Union Guard Member from Chicago, IL
Schafer, Henry (35)
Schneider, Henry (NA) — IN #45
Scolian, James (33) — Union Guard Member
Seibert, B. Fredrick (47) — IN #135
Sentfleben, Henry (29) — IN #23
Sheehy, James (33) — IN #113, AM
Shehan, Bridget (NA)
Sherrod, John (NA) — IN #139
Silk, Amelia (18)

Simpson, George L. (NA)	from Joliet, IL
Slaughter, Thomas (32)	IN #34, Crew-
	from Milwaukee, WI
Smith, Charles (NA)	from Chicago, IL
Smith, James (NA)	
Sneider, Phillip (NA)	
Spellane, Mary (22)	IN #86, AM
Spellane, Michael (15)	IN #161, AM
Sullivan, Ellen (NA)	from Chicago, IL
Sullivan, Jeremiah (46)	
Sullivan, Mary (NA)	IN #49
Tevlin, James (20)	
Tevlin, Jane (22)	
Thomas, Jeremiah (NA)	IN #36
	Crew-from Chicago, IL
Veale (Vail), James (32)	AM
Waegli, Samuel (30)	Register of Deeds
Wagner, John (NA)	from Philadelphia, PA
Waldo, Edwin (26)	IN #60
	from Ontonagon, MI
Walker, Emily (45)	from Chicago, IL
Wallace, W.H. (25)	Crew-Drover
Walradt, O.H. (NA)	
Ward, Mary (22)	IN #6
Weaver, Michael (23)	
Weiskoff, Henry (35)	
Williams, Allan (28)	
Williams, Theresa Ellen (30)	AM
Wilson, Jack (NA)	IN #73, Coldwater, MI
	Captain of *Lady Elgin*
Wilson, William (37)	
Woods, Thomas (23)	

Bibliography

Internet Sources

Archdiocese of Milwaukee Catholic Cemeteries, "Self-Guided Tour of Historical Calvary Cemetery," http://www.cemeteries.org/Catholic-Cemeteries/PDF1/CalvarySelfGuidedTour_Final.pdf (accessed December 2017)

Baillod, Brendan, "The Wreck of the Steamer Lady Elgin," http://www.ship-wrecks.net/shipwreck/projects/elgin/ (accessed December 2017)

Chicagology, "Lady Elgin," https://chicagology.com/notorious-chicago/ladyelgin/ (accessed December, 2017)

Clark, Wes, "The Story of Edward W. Spencer," http://wesclark.com/burbank/did_i_do_my_best.html (accessed December, 2017)

Gurda, John, "Lost on the Lady Elgin: A new account emerges," http://archive.jsonline.com/news/opinion/104189029.html/ (accessed November, 2017)

Jastrzembski, Frank, "This Union General cheated death twice before the Civil War even started," http://www.wearethemighty.com/articles/this-union-general-cheated-death-twice-before-the-civil-war-even-started (accessed November 2017)

Maritime History of the Great Lakes, "Lady Elgin (Steamboat), sunk by collision, 8 Sep 1860," http://images.maritimehistoryofthegreatlakes.ca/41880/data (accessed November 2017)

Milwaukee County Wisconsin Genealogy, "Lake Michigan Shipwrecks and Disasters," http://www.linkstothepast.com/milwaukee/marinedis.php (accessed November 2017)

New York Times, September 10, 1860, "Fearful Disaster on Lake Michigan," http://www.nytimes.com/1860/09/10/news/fearful-disaster-lake-michigan-steamer-lady-elgin-sunk-collision-with-schooner.html?pagewanted=all (accessed December 2017)

PBS, "Rising Wind: The Lady Elgin Story," http://www.pbs.org/show/rising-wind-lady-elgin-story/ (accessed October 2017)

Pisacreta, Sharon, "Doomed by the Lake; The Lady Elgin and The Augusta," http://www.lakeeffectliving.com/Oct11/Shipwrecks-LadyElgin-Augusta.html (accessed December 2017)

Shipwreck Explorers, "Steamer Lady Elgin," https://www.shipwreckexplorers.com/steamer-lady-elgin/ (accessed December 2017)

Winnetka Historical Society, "Death on Lake Michigan: The Lady Elgin Tragedy," http://www.winnetkahistory.org/gazette/death-on-lake-michigan-the-lady-elgin-tragedy/ (accessed December 2017)

Winnetka Historical Society, "What Brought the Lady Elgin to Chicago," http://www.winnetkahistory.org/gazette/what-brought-the-lady-elgin-to-chicago/ (accessed October 2017)

Wisconsin Historical Markers, "Marker 327:Sinking of the Lady Elgin," http://www.wisconsinhistoricalmarkers.com/2012/08/marker-327-sinking-of-lady-elgin.html (accessed (November 2017)

Wisconsin Historical Society, "Odd Wisconsin: Nearly 300 Drowned in Lady Elgin Disaster," http://lacrossetribune.com/couleecourier/lifestyles/odd-wisconsin-nearly-drowned-in-lady-elgin-wreck/article_3643d4d1-0283-5463-b66b-1acef153ae87.html (accessed December 2017)

Wisconsin Historical Society, "Historical Essay: Lady Elgin (shipwreck, 1860), https://www.wisconsinhistory.org/Records/Article/CS1797 (accessed December 2017)

Books

Atwater, F. *Atwater History and Genealogy, Volume 1,* 1998

Bourrie, Mark, *Many a Midnight Ship: True Stories of the Great Lakes Shipwrecks,* Ann Arbor, MI: University of Michigan Press, 2005

Cathedral of St. John the Baptist, *History of the Cathedral Parish*

Mansfield, John B. *History of the Great Lakes,* Chicago: JH Beers and Company, 1899

Matteson, Clark S., *History of Wisconsin: From Prehistoric to Present Periods,* Milwaukee, WI: Milwaukee Historical Publishing Company, 1893

Ratigan, William, *Great Lakes Shipwrecks and Survivals,* Grand Rapids, MI: William B. Eerdman's Publishing Company, 1960

Scanlan, Charles Martin, *The Lady Elgin Disaster:September 8, 1860,* Milwaukee: Cannon Printing Company, 1928

Van Heest, Valerie, *Lost on the Lady Elgin,* United States: In-Depth Editions, 2010

Archives

Calvary Cemetery (Holy Cross)

Christ Church, Winnetka, IL

Forest Home Cemetery

Milwaukee Historical Society

Random Lake Historical Society

Richfield (WI) Historical Society

Sheboygan County Historical Society

ALLISON,

HAPPY IRISH FEST 2019!

BEST WISHES,

Paul
Hollander

"BORN FREE, LIVE FREE, RIDE FREE!"

Made in the USA
Lexington, KY
04 July 2019